"OH, MY GOD, THEY'RE EVERYWHERE!"

A scream in his headset and a hysterically protracted burst of automatic weapons fire.

In about half a second a tidal wave of light crashed across Billy McKay's field of vision to the accompaniment of shattering noise. He saw dark figures come apart before his very eyes as hundreds of steel marbles tore through them. Rogers had triggered the Claymores set in a swastika pattern around the huts.

Screams of wounded intruders began to filter through the ringing the Claymores had left in his ears.

A shriek in his headset almost tore his head off. The artificial light was strobing erratically as the flare began to gutter out. He saw bodies littering the hard-packed earth . . .

THE GUARDIANS series
from Jove

THE GUARDIANS
VALLEY OF THE GODS

RICHARD AUSTIN

JOVE BOOKS, NEW YORK

THE GUARDIANS: VALLEY OF THE GODS

A Jove Book / published by arrangement with
the author

PRINTING HISTORY
Jove edition / August 1988

ISBN: 0-515-09642-3

PRINTED IN THE UNITED STATES OF AMERICA

10 9 8 7 6 5 4 3 2 1

For Mike Weaver

For Hospitality

PROLOGUE

The roar of the crowd broke over Luis Portero like surf as he raised his arms. Dawn light stained the voluminous white sleeves of his robe like wine.

He spread his hands. Hush fell like a single great door across the multitude. For a moment he stood there and simply watched adoration beat from the upturned faces, alight beneath the butter glow of dawn.

"My children," he said, deliberately putting a touch of the peasant into his Spanish. The microphone clipped to the simple collar of his robe, above the glory that surrounded the head of the Virgin, picked up his words; the big speakers to either side of the dais unfurled them over the horde like banners.

He felt their joy answer him, felt it as he felt the rumbling of the generator that powered the sound system through the tire-rubber soles of his sandals.

He began to speak the day's blessing. It wasn't Mass, wasn't anything consecrated by the hierarchy of the Roman church in which he and every one of his listeners had been raised. It came instead from his heart, and he had no doubt he was inspired by the Holy Spirit as he spoke.

As the words poured out of him a synthesized drumbeat throbbed beneath them, volume and tempo modulated by a technician crouching behind the platform with a headset over his ears. It caught the massed heartbeat of his listeners and dragged them along, filling their bodies with excitement as their souls quickened with the Spirit.

Once, in an earlier life, Father Luis Portero, SJ, had held a degree in clinical psych from the Sorbonne, and a Harvard MBA. To him there was nothing incongruous about using stage magic and cutting-edge advertising techniques to fire up the faithful. The Jesuits had never been averse to giving the Holy Ghost a little help now and then. Though the revelations of Sister Light had made him turn his back on his old order, he still had a lot of the Company in him.

Besides, he told himself, *we've suffered a terrible setback at the hands of the* ateos. The faithful would need all their strength to press on, to carry the holy war deep into the underbelly of the godless empire of *America del norte.*

For a moment Casey Wilson allowed himself to be aware of the little patch of South Texas hardpan pressing against him from below. He felt its hardness, the nocturnal cool of it seeping into belly and thighs. He let his mind focus on the sensual, animal pleasure of it; of the rustle and velvet caress of the dawn breeze, and the moist spring tang of the sparse ground cover.

He took pleasure in the picture: from the black of a velvet painting background moments ago the sky was now shading subtly to indigo. The wide land about him was beginning to take on definition, hills and sharp-cut arroyos softened by the gray promise of light, sandy soil that looked in the gloom to be the color and texture of fine wood ash dotted with scrub. In a few more minutes the gray would start to go lavender, and then the heights and the tips of branches and shoots of winter-dry grass would catch alight with the first beaten-brass glow of the sun.

From almost a mile away the drum synthesizer beat up into him like the heartbeat of the earth. He knew it was manipulating him, knew it was tuning his pulse to the beating of ten thousand hearts. He let it. Let it erode the interfering self from behind the yellow lenses of his Zeiss shooting glasses, let it carry him into the Zen mode of *no thought, no intention*.

He felt false dawn rising behind him. Soon the sun would come.

"My Children," Portero said. His voice reverberated around the amphitheater-like valley, a bowl full of people. "Let your hearts fill with joy! Even as I speak to you, our Little Sister Light is preparing her triumphal entry into the capital of our holy land."

He waited for the cheers to subside. "Great are the sacrifices that will be demanded of you. But what is life, what is hardship, compared to the promise of heaven? You are peasants, sons and daughters of the soil. You know that life is hardship. And you know a saint's crown awaits you in heaven.

"But now you know this, as well: if we fall, others will rise up behind us, and others, on and on, to bear the revelations of Sister Light abroad and drown the heretics in blood and fire!"

The image of the man on the distant dais wavered gently before Casey's eyes. He didn't take the swimming too seriously. At the magnification he was using, the slightest movement would jog the picture, even the shifting of wind, or involuntary motions so minor they couldn't be suppressed by his yoga deep-breathing discipline.

The scope was a miracle of hot-superconductor technology. The faint predawn light was collected and then refined by marvelous nanoprocessors into the image projected on the lens in front of Casey's right eye. It gave him the same see-through capacity on the fine optical sight the system was built around that the head-up display in the cockpit of his old F-16 used to provide; he could ignore the fancy high-tech stuff, or turn it off completely to rely only on ground-glass lenses and his fighter-ace's eyesight, without shifting the sight picture by a second of arc.

He watched him, the far-away man in the white robe with the painting on the front, trying to catch the rhythms of his motions. Fortunately, he wasn't the sort of orator who strutted around the stage a lot, like the televangelists Casey'd grown up making fun of on Saturday afternoons in southern California. He kept his feet planted, though the loose sleeves of his robe flapped like wings as he gestured. Good; it was harder than almost anybody realized to hit a human being moving at random over even a very small area, even at very short range. To say nothing of a range at which most marksmen would consider themselves lucky to get a shot into a ten foot circle that wasn't going anywhere.

The universe collapsed around him until there was only him and the man on the platform. The restless mob of the faithful were gone, his three teammates hunkered down at a discreet distance to pull security for him ceased to exist. It all came down to two.

At last the feeling was right. Without thinking about it Casey drew a breath deep down into his belly, pulling with his diaphragm. The man on the dais touched both hands to his heart, to the painting of the Virgin of Guadalupe as seen by the Indian Juan Diego four centuries before. Casey let half the breath out, caught it. His finger tightened fractionally on the taut trigger. It broke like a dry twig.

The sound of the shot came to him as if from a great distance.

"Today, my children," Luis Juan Portero shouted, "today we strike!" And he flung his arms out in an embrace that took in the multitude.

The 180-grain jacketed bullet slid down the far side of its long arc and punched through the printed face of the Virgin of Guadalupe, through skin and ribs to pulp the heart behind with the last of the energy that had brought it across fourteen hundred meters. It didn't exit from his back.

Luis Portero went straight down the way a heart-shot man does, onto his back with his arms outspread like a crucifix. No one heard the shot, masked by a sound suppressor and the crowd's exuberance.

It was as if he'd been stuck down by the hand of God. When his bodyguards reached him his eyes were open and the image on his chest had been blotted out by blood.

CHAPTER
ONE

"Everything is in readiness, comrade," the man said across the spotted linen tablecloth. "Your plan is succeeding brilliantly."

Silviano Orozco Ituarte took a gulp of coffee as if he had to bite it off. It must have been very hot; the late winter sun played warm on the sidewalk café at the fringes of Mexico City's crowded Zocalo, but not hot enough to bring the sweat in beads to his high balding forehead like that.

Colonel Ivan Vesensky almost permitted himself to smile at the crude attempt at flattery. This arrogant little toad no doubt thought himself the cleverest son of a bitch in the valley of Mexico for the way he was manipulating his powerful ally from across the sea into believing that this scheme was his. Whereas, of course, the whole breathtakingly brilliant plan had hatched from the prominent forehead of himself, Silviano Orozco Ituarte, acting secretary general of the Revolutionary Action Movement.

As a matter of cold fact, the plan *was* Vesensky's, and it was Orozco who had been tricked into imagining he'd thought it all up himself. There were still a few details he wasn't aware of.

They'd come clear in time, Vesensky was sure. Mexicans thought all foreigners were fools. They were right, too, as a general rule. But not in the specific case of Ivan Vesensky.

"I'm pleased," he murmured in English. His Spanish wasn't very good. Then again, he hadn't exactly let on to knowing any at all.

Orozco's head bobbed up and down inside the crumpled open collar of the shirt he wore beneath a tweed sports coat with suede patches at the elbows. Moist protuberant eyes blinked rapidly, appreciatively.

"Our elite hit teams have neutralized key leaders of the reactionary unions who've been holding out on us, *Señor* Victor" Orozco hit the cover name hard, just in case Vesensky had forgotten he knew it *was* a cover. It was important to impress this blond foreigner with the designer clothes and ski-instructor build in every way possible. Because he wasn't just the Anglo-Saxon journalist he appeared. He had the power to make Orozco President of Mexico.

"Our student groups have been rioting for two weeks, and by themselves have the provisional government teetering. When we throw in widespread strikes—" A meaningful glance at the bulky National Palace on the eastern side of the vast square, which had originally been built from the rubble of Moctezuma's palace and sort of jumbled onto since. Inside it leaders of half a dozen major factions, would-be successors to the Aztec First Speaker—or his conqueror—were jockeying for ascendancy. "What chance do the bourgeois pretenders to the throne have, I ask you?"

"The *Cristero* army squatting north of town might have a little to do with it, too, don't you think?" Vesensky asked, his tone dry as a James Bond martini.

Orozco acknowledged the possibility with a shrug.

"A stroke of good fortune that Córdoba died, no?" he said, pitching his voice low so the rest of the midmorning crowd wouldn't hear. "He was too popular, that one."

Vesensky nodded. Actually, it had been an elementary two-hundred-meter shot with a black-market rifle that had done for

Mexico's recently deceased president. Fortune had nothing to do with it. Ivan Vesensky wasn't one to rely on luck when it came to a business as touchy as assassination.

A twinge from inside his pink Yves Saint-Laurent shirt made him smile. *Except when the assassination in question is my own,* he thought. If he hadn't moved at an opportune millisecond, the bullet fired by Guardian Casey Wilson would have left him dead on a balcony in the ruins of Washington, D.C. six months before.

Orozco caught Vesensky's smile, made it his own and turned it around. He leaned forward and slapped the sleeve of Vesensky's white linen jacket expansively. Vesensky forced himself not to recoil. "Well, then, well," Orozco said, raising his cup. "A toast to . . . friends from abroad."

Vesensky relaxed. For a moment he'd been afraid the fool was going to blurt the letters *KGB*. That wouldn't have been good at all. He smiled thinly and hoisted his glass of mineral water in reply.

Orozco smacked his lips and wiped them with his sleeve. "So," he said, leaning forward. "Once we make our move, you'll be able to support us?" He rolled his eyes conspiratorily around in his head, accenting his unfortunate resemblance to Cheech Marin.

"Of course."

"We always knew the imperialists couldn't beat you," Orozco said, settling back. "I read those books they printed in English: *Soviet War Plans.* How thermonuclear war was just part of your strategy to destroy the imperialists and their running-dog lackeys." His eyes glittered like obsidian marbles. "They said you had been destroyed. I knew it was a lie. And now you're ready to bring the revolution to the very heartland of capitalist repression."

"Indeed," Vesensky said solemnly, in that well-bred but not stuffy British accent he used as part of his cover. Inside he was laughing. *We couldn't win in Afghanistan or Iran. In 1980 we couldn't even* invade *Poland. And now he thinks we're about to come swarming up out of the surf with our hammers and sickles in hand to pound the North Americans into shape! He must have seen* Red Dawn *fifteen times as a child.*

"But now," Vesensky said, "let's discuss a more immediate form of support." He swung a slim briefcase up onto the table. Orozco was about to start orating. Aside from the fact Vesensky's central nervous system wasn't up to that, he didn't want every other patron and all the staff of the sidewalk café to suspect he was anything but British reporter Ian Victor.

He opened the case in Orozco's face. Even the thin light filtering through the high haze splashed back onto Orozco's chipmunk cheeks in a mellow yellow glow. Or maybe that was Vesensky's imagination; *he* had seen *Raiders of the Lost Ark* five times, himself. But there was no mistaking the rapt, almost devout expression on the face of the leader of Mexico's Armed Revolutionary Movement.

Orozco reached out a soft ring-bedecked hand. Aspirant terrorists who came to the special camps in the Soviet Union and client states like North Korea and South Yemen generally had soft bourgeois hands, not horny proletarian hands; Vesensky had observed that often enough during his stints as an instructor. When they left their hands were calloused, of course. Surprising what a short time they took to soften again.

Orozco picked up a one-ounce gold coin inlaid with the hammer-and-sickle and Cyrillic writing and held it close to his nose, as if he'd forgotten to put on his contact lenses. The sweat-domes popped out afresh on his forehead like mushrooms after a rain. *"Santa María,"* he breathed.

Vensensky nodded judiciously. "You should be able to do yourself a lot of good with that," he said, plucking the lime slice from the rim of his glass and biting out the pulp. "In terms of suborning capitalist lackeys, that is."

Don't be too arch, he warned himself. He didn't want to risk stoking Orozco's dim flicker of consciousness into any flares of suspicion. Not now.

Deft as a magician forcing a card on an insurance salesman in a leisure suit, Vesensky snapped the briefcase out of Orozco's hand and closed. He locked it ostentatiously, placed it on the red brick flagging at his feet. He slid the key across the tablecloth at Orozco, throwing up a tiny bow wave of spilled salt.

With equal adroitness Orozco made the coin disappear, picked up the key, and slipped it into a pocket. He dropped his eyes as if they could bore through red and white checkered cloth and the wood beneath it to the briefcase. He could feel it burning by his leg like a miniature sun; Vesensky read it from his eyes.

Vesensky stood. "I'll be in touch."

Distracted, Orozco nodded. He was still staring a hole in the tablecloth.

"Remember to wait five minutes before you leave. It wouldn't do for people to suspect you were under foreign influence, now, would it?"

That brought Orozco's head up; if it were suspected he was taking bribes from foreign agents, in the current overheated political climate the very best he could hope for was to be decently shot, instead of, say, ripped limb from limb by a mob.

Vesensky touched a slim finger to his brow. *"Adios."*

Orozco swallowed. *"Vaya con Dios."*

Walking away across a street clogged with slow-moving cars in spite of the recent reduction in gas rations, Vesensky smiled. *Irony,* he thought. *I didn't think you had it in you, Silviano, old chap.* He took a black plastic object of the size and general appearance of a hand calculator from his jacket pocket and began punching the keys.

A hundred yards away he stopped and looked back across the plaza. Orozco sat craning his neck while trying desperately not to show it. He looked like nothing so much as a man who had just sold his country to a foreign power for a briefcase full of gold.

Mexico had never been any better for the *Komitet Gosudarstvennoi Bezopasnosti.* In 1971 a Soviet-backed scheme to destabilize Mexico was blown up in the face of the State Security Committee by the loudmouthed *machismo* of the very same *Movimiento de Acción Revolucionario* that Orozco now headed. Twenty-five years later senior KGB officers couldn't mention Mexico without a shudder and a look over the shoulder. It had contributed enormously to Vesensky's mystique within the *Komitet* that he was able to maintain a functional network of contacts within that troublesome country.

He'd been able to do so by playing on the vanity and limitations of fools such as Orozco. He never *expected* his puppets to be anything but zealots, loons, and venal swine, which gave him an edge over his fellow operatives in the KGB—and his opposite numbers in the CIA, for that matter.

But for all his avarice, Orozco was a true believer in his strange Stalinist vision. He really imagined that the KGB was about to help him liberate his squalid little country.

What a pity, Ivan Vesensky thought, *that I betrayed the KGB while it was still a viable organization.*

He pressed a final button.

There was a flash as blocks of plastic explosive blew the layer of gold coins which had concealed them out in a lethal glittering fan.

For a moment Vesensky stood and watched as smoldering bits of debris settled into the ruins of the sidewalk café. Out on the plaza people were picking themselves up and pointing with exclamations of horror. Some of the ones nearest the café rolled on the ground clutching themselves and moaning.

Orozco had been a useful tool. He had played a role in preventing a strong government from emerging to succeed the murdered Córdoba, no doubt of that. But once that was accomplished his belief that he was meant to come to power made him inconvenient. Fatally so.

Those ridiculously unsubtle coins that had gone into the world's most costly claymore mine—specially minted in the Federated States of Europe not four weeks ago—would prove to the xenophobic Mexican public that the MAR had once again sold out to the USSR, shredding the radical movement's reputation as thoroughly as they had Orozco and a dozen or so other patrons of the café.

People were streaming past him, avid for catastrophe. Somewhere sirens went *doo-wah,* sounding for all the world like robots trying to imitate the background vocals to a Fifties song. Vesensky hyperventilated for a moment, swallowed rapidly several times, to get the blown-away look appropriate to a weak-stomached *gringo* tourist confronted by a little too much Mexican reality. He began to breast the stream of the curious, stumbling, handkerchief to mouth. No point in hanging around waiting for some keen-eyed soul to remember seeing him in the café moments before the blast.

Inside he exulted. The attempt to seize the seawater desalinization facility near Houston had ended in disaster, as he had predicted it would. The orange-haired bit of French fluff who had replaced him as Chairman Maximov's chief adviser was too hung up on the Blueprint for Renewal, and at her insistence the Chairman had forced Vesensky to overextend himself.

But the damage wasn't fatal. And the real work of the *Cristero* uprising he had done so much to foster was about to be accomplished here, in the ancient valley of Mexico, the valley of the gods.

CHAPTER
TWO ─────────────

"I definitely admire the way your tits ride up your rib cage when you do that," Billy McKay said with a standard-issue shit-eating grin.

Eyes the blue of the South Texas sky flashed at him from a considerable height off the hardwood bedroom floor. "Is that any way to talk to a lady?" Lt. Col. Marla Eklund of the Army of the Republic of Texas asked frostily. "Watch your language, you Yankee son of a bitch."

"It's the way I talk to a lady when she's doing her stretching exercises stark naked in the presence of a strange man. Do I know your name, lady?"

" 'Strange man' is right. I'm Belle Starr."

"I thought she was a great big dyke who looked like Gertrude Stein."

"Where the hell did you ever hear about Gertrude Stein? I didn't think you ever read anything but old Marvel comics."

"Shit, I don't even read those. Make it a policy never to read nothing that hasn't got any tit in it." He locked his fingers behind the invisibly short blond hair at the back of his thick neck and glanced at the window. A louver of sunlight glowed through the venetian blind. "Sam Sloan told me about Gertrude Stein. Matter of fact, what he told me about her was that Belle Starr looked like her in a cowboy suit. That and that she was another dyke, with a girlfriend even uglier than she was."

He cocked an eye at Eklund. "Say, is there something you ain't telling me? I kind of wondered if you ever had a man before, as shy and inexperienced as you was acting . . . "

Eklund uncoiled her elbow from behind her neck and gave McKay the finger. "Eat this, Yankee."

He showed her a grin and swung off the bed. "Negative on that. I see something else I'd like, though."

He sauntered up to her, with his dick kind of unfurling as it swung between his muscular thighs. She backed up until her ass bumped the edge of a dresser.

"Back off, bluebelly. I gotta do my exercise." She was barely three inches shorter than he was, and he was six-three.

He put a hand on a full breast, rolled a nipple between thumb and forefinger. "This is exercise."

She tried to push him away. But her nipple was standing up now, pink and just glowing. "Get off," she said.

"That's the plan." He reached a hand down between her legs, stroked a finger along her pussy, brought it up and around and around. She looked at him and bit her lip, and her eyes got big and round and shiny.

"*Damn* you," she said huskily. Her legs were long, almost as long as his, with the sculpted, just-padded muscularity of a weight-lifter. She cocked one of those legs around the small of his back and drew him forward as he entered her.

Later, in the kitchen of Eklund's tract home, Billy McKay sat sipping coffee from a heavy earthenware mug. It was fresh coffee, made from beans run up from Central America across the Gulf of Mexico. It tasted good.

He gazed out the window. The view beyond frilly curtains that didn't suit his former drill sergeant hostess *at all* was jarring: a couple of wall studs, black and covered with bumps of char, sticking up against a low-overcast sky. Burnt-out tract houses climbed the rocky hills farther along. The northern outskirts of San Antontio had been thoroughly trashed by warheads targeted for Randolph Air Force Base; the little house

Eklund had been given as part of her contract with the Republic had been spared by one of those freaks of blast dynamics and reflection of the thermal flash. The character of the neighborhood didn't seem to bother Marla much—like a lot of Texicans McKay had encountered, she took "don't fence me in" fairly seriously. Still, to McKay the contrast between the homey little kitchen and the devastation outside was a bit freaky, hardened though he was.

Marla was making breakfast at the stove, which burned methane bottled at a plant in New Braunfels—a pure post-Holocaust operation. She was wearing a fatigue shirt. The tail of it left a tempting white slice of each well-muscled ass cheek bare.

"Hear about ol' Randy Jim?" she asked, scrambling eggs with tomatoes, onion, and chile. "Came on the radio while you were in the bathroom scraping the fungus off your face."

McKay grunted.

"He turned up in Okie City asking for asylum from our good buddy Reverend Forrie. Forrie welcomed him with open arms."

"Jesus."

It made a certain kind of sense. Randall James Hedison was the last elected governor of the State of Texas, and after the One-Day War he maintained lip-service loyalty to the United States, in pious contrast to the secessionist Republic. But he refused to respond to the *Cristero* threat, and when the *Cristeros* made their drive on the Blueprint desalinization plant he'd done his part—by launching attacks against the Republic all along the border, preventing the Texicans from relieving a beleaguered force consisting of the four Guardians, Texas Republican volunteers, and Northern Mexican refugees driven from their farms by the *Cristero* swarms.

To be so bold Randy Jim had to have backing in the Washington rubble, and not just from the alliance of street gangs and rubble runners the Guardians had forged to protect the returned president. Like his buddies, McKay suspected Hedison's old crony Dr. Marguerite Connoly, the onetime Harvard economist and self-appointed chief of the White House staff of encouraging the governor, she hated the idea of session—and she hated the Guardians more.

No matter what support Hedison thought he had for his hand,

though, he'd overplayed it, defying a direct demand by President Jeffrey MacGregor to cease hostilities and help the Republic turn back the invasion. Infuriated by the arrogance of the Texas Rangers, whom Hedison had expanded into a corps of personal storm troopers, and rankling at having to watch Texan soil overrun by the *Cristeros,* the Texas Federal military—who, after all, were still nominally part of the U.S. armed forces—declared martial law, besieged Hedison and his Ranger bodyguards in the gigantic SAURON Tower in Dallas, and sent air strikes to smash the *Cristero* army that ringed in the Bernardo de Galves Experimental Seawater Desalinization Facility.

It was mutiny, beyond question. Treason, in point of fact. The problem was *whose.*

The Federal Texan forces claimed they were serving their commander in chief, and that Governor Hedison's acts constituted lending aid and comfort to the enemy. That may or may not have given them power to depose a duly elected civilian authority—but, while Billy McKay still thought Jeff MacGregor could be kind of a liberal wimp at times, the President had taken too much grief in his quest to assert his authority and reunify a nation splintered by war to quibble over legalisms.

What Maggie Connoly thought was a matter of conjecture—which the Guardians had duly made, at length and profanely, during the hell-bending alcohol-drenched celebration that followed the Texican relief force Republican President Lamar Louis Napoleon LaRousse led through the gates of the Galves plant. Centralization of authority in President MacGregor's hands was one of her big goals—and she was responsible for administering the Blueprint for Renewal, the top-secret pre-war plan for rebuilding America's technological, industrial, and economic base, of which the Galves plant was a component. In the words of one of her predecessors in the White House, she had no choice but to let her boy Randall James twist slowly in the wind.

Randy Jim, his cabinet, and the Ranger command vanished from his headquarters, apparently through utility tunnels underground. Now the governor had apparently turned up again, knocking on the door of former boy-wonder televangelist Nathan Bedford Forrest Smith.

McKay cocked a suspicious eyebrow at Eklund. ''You listening to KFSU?'' That was the megawatt radio station that broadcast from Nathan Bedford Forrest Smith University in Oklahoma, central citadel of the most obvious cancer growing in the body of a recovering America.

"Sure. Since the FCC banned shock radio, it's the funniest thing on the air, mornings."

McKay grunted again. At least Eklund'd had the decency to turn that shit off before he came out of the crapper. Alone, it seemed, in North America, the Guardians failed to see the humor in Reverend Forrie's overwrought broadcasts. Of course, compared to Smith, Maggie Connoly was the Guardians' fairy godmother. The Guardians had wrecked a major crusade by the Church of the New Dispensation, to which Smith was the loudest convert, and in the process wrecked the Church's First Prophet, the radiation-resistant and thoroughly loony Josiah Coffin. Since then their relationship with Forrie had gone progressively downhill.

"We're gonna have to do something about that cocksucker," McKay said. "He was in with Coffin, he backed the Effsees when they were occupyin' us, and now this. Where the hell are those eggs?"

Eklund whirled with a plate in one hand and a scoopful of scrambled eggs in the other. "Right there, you Yankee son of a bitch!" she shouted, and slammed the eggs at the plate. They splashed.

"Hey, what's the matter—aw, shit." McKay dabbed frantically at his eye with his napkin. A bit of egg with chile had hit him there. It burned like tear gas. "What'd I say?"

Eklund was trying to unfasten the short apron tied around her waist, doing things to her shirttail that would have been very interesting under other circumstances. "Nothin'. I'm just the waitress and short-order cook at this here roadside diner. Well, Goddamn it all to hell anyway." She took the strap in both hands and broke it with a heave of her shoulders.

McKay's eye was tearing furiously. His other eye started to weep in sympathy, or maybe he'd gotten some chile into it in his struggles. "Now, just a godamned minute here. Ow, ah. I didn't mean anything, I was just kidding, goddamn it, can't you take a joke—"

She threw the apron down and stomped out.

McKay reeled to the sink. Water pressure was up this morning. He splashed cold water in his face until the stinging in his eyes subsided. Then he dabbed scrambled-egg shrapnel off his OD T-shirt.

The bedroom door slammed. McKay saw Eklund flash by, wearing gray warmup pants, a white South Padre Island souvenir T-shirt, and New Balance running shoes. She went out the front door without ever looking back.

McKay picked up the plate, sat down at the table, and began to eat.

Before he finished, his pocket calculator-sized communicator beeped for attention. He padded back into the bedroom and picked it up.

It was Tom Rogers, telling his commander in his polite way that he was to shag ass downtown *muy pronto*. The ex-Green Beret had no details, but McKay got that tightening in the base of his nut-sac that told him action was about to happen.

So soon? a voice inside of him asked. It seemed like only yesterday old LaRousse had come rolling through the gates of the Galves plant with his white mane streaming out behind him.

And a little part of him thought about the little soap opera he'd just acted out with Marla Eklund, and it said, *about goddamned time*.

The man in the polo shirt flashed a Naugahyde smile across the table at the Guardians. "I'm only here as a briefing officer, of course. Not part of your chain of command. Wouldn't want to poach in Dr. J's territory."

"Who?" McKay asked.

Former CIA agent Ronald FitzSimmons blinked. He was an empty-eyed preppy, the type who would've been portrayed in movies before the war by Gary Busey, when he wasn't singing about Pretty Peggy Sue and getting mashed into the planet along with Richie Valens and the Big Bopper. "Why, your new CO. Dr. Jake."

"Dr. Morgenstern, I guess you mean," Sam Sloan said in his best Jim Garner hick deadpan.

"Uh. Yes. That's right." His eyes clicked from Sloan to McKay, detent to detent. A little bitty vee spoiled the sunlamp-

tanned perfection of his forehead. He glanced down at the notebook computer open on the table before him.

Sloan and McKay rolled their eyes at each other. They spent a lot of time at odds. At the moment, though, they were in perfect accord.

"What exactly is it you have for us, Mr. FitzSimmons?" Tom Rogers asked, prodding gently in that calm, quiet way of his. He was sitting to the side with both feet on the floor, square hands on his thighs.

"Ah. Well." He dabbed at the keys of his computer. "As you know, the Portero touch was an unqualified success."

Sloan grimaced. He thought "touch" was the smarmiest euphemism for "assassination"—or murder, if you like—that had yet come down the pike. McKay misread his meaning, took out his cigar, and tipped it to him in front of a nasty smirk. Sloan hadn't been enthusiastic about the killing. McKay, of course, thought it was balls.

"As we and our friends here in the, uh, Republic—" He stumbled over that; he was in Connoly's cadre, and no friend of secession. On the other hand, the Company wasn't known for being choosy as to who it dealt with. "As we predicted, the disorganization factor arising from the death of the ablest of the *Cristero* field leaders outweighed the martyrdom element. The invading forces are in disarray, and don't for one minute think we in Washington are oblivious to the debt of gratitude we owe Lieutenant Wilson here."

He looked at Casey and tried on the smile again. Slick, shiny, artificial, and worthless. Naugahyde. Casey just sat fiddling with a yellow felt-tip pen, turning it over and over in his long, strong fingers, pulling it open, popping it back together, intent as if it were a Rubik's cube. He didn't acknowledge the smile.

Sloan wondered what was going on behind the yellow-tinted lenses of the former fighter pilot's Zeiss glasses. Did he think about the ramifications of destroying a human life without giving the victim a chance to fight back, or had the Portero kill just been another problem in dynamic geometry to him, like figuring deflection in air-to-air combat? During the years of little war that were prelude to the Big One, Wilson had pulled off the only five-kill mission of the Jet Age. He was a private person, as unknowable in his own way as Tom Rogers, who was as outgoing as a cinderblock—not like McKay, or Sam himself, who tended to be very upfront and let all the world know what they were feeling. But Sam had the idea Casey preferred the clean competition of war in the air, where you could best a man by wrecking his machine instead of necessarily killing him.

And where you never had to look your victim in the eye as your shots went home.

The lines of his mouth hardened a touch. If McKay knew what he was thinking he'd ride him unmercifully; he had a hell of a lot of right to look down on Casey for preferring an impersonal style of war, when as a gunnery officer he used to deal out destruction from inside the metal guts of the cruiser *Winston-Salem*.

FitzSimmons looked at Casey for an expectant beat. Then he went on. "But the *Cristero* collapse all along the line of contact isn't just attributable to the Lieutenant's fine marksmanship, nor the unceasing military efforts of the Republican and loyal Texan forces."

It was a calculated dig. And probably a wasted one; Sam Sloan would've bet money their Texican hosts hadn't bothered to bug the briefing room they'd lent them in the San Antonio city hall, a glass box that had lost its upper stories to the bombing and which served as the center of Republican government. He found himself deploring the lax security of it even as he applauded the principle. *I've been hanging around McKay too long.*

McKay stuck a cigar in his mouth, scratched a wooden kitchen match alight with his thumbnail. It was a trick he'd picked up from Dreadlock Callahan. "You mean," he asked, puffing the cigar alight, "they ain't runnin' away 'cause we're kicking their asses?"

Ever so briefly FitzSimmons allowed himself to look pained. He was one of those college jock types who looked on the body as the temple of the spirit or whatever the hell. And you could bet that in Maggie Connoly's Washington there was no smoking in government meeting rooms, even if the ashes of a hundred thousand human beings incinerated by thermonuclear explosions were still clinging to the carpet and caked on the filing cabinets.

"That's part of it, of course. But recent events in Mexico lead our analysts to believe there's more to it than that."

McKay crossed his thick arms over his chest. "Such as?"

"As you're aware, the charismatic and very popular President Enrique Córdoba of Mexico was assassinated by a sniper some weeks ago, in much the same way as Lieutenant Wilson dealt with the *Cristero* leader Portero."

Casey frowned slightly, as if wondering whether he was being blamed for that.

"Shortly thereafter, the *Cristero* movement cropped up again in San Luis Potosí. It was considered to be a predictable effect of the anarchy that gripped the country after the death of the man who had held it together in the wake of the One-Day War, especially given the fortuitous emergence of a seventeen-year-old prophetess, a virgin of course"—grin—"who called herself *Hermana Luz,* or Sister Light. Irruptions of this sort have been common through much of Mexican history. The current set of fanatics openly style themselves after the religious zealots who fought the government under the name *Cristeros* during the Twenties and Thirties.

"But you gentlemen yourselves turned up evidence that led us to question the obvious conclusions."

He sat there smirking expectantly. It was Casey who got it. "Vesensky!" he exclaimed, and actually snapped his fingers.

"You've got it. Colonel Ivan Vesensky, formerly of the KGB, now FSE Chairman Maximov's chief manipulator. And chief assassin."

"So you figure Vesensky greased this Córdoba dude to get things stirred up so he could spring this *Cristero* shit," McKay said. He scowled. Much as he hated to admit it, FitzSimmons was making sense. "Okay, fine. What's that got to do with why these Soldiers of Christ crazies are pulling back now?"

"Our sources tell us a substantial number of *Cristeros* have appeared on the northern outskirts of Mexico City, where any number of factions are still jockeying to see who will replace Córdoba." He spread his hands on the table before him. "Do I really have to make it any clearer?"

Casey whistled.

"A power vacuum, a charismatic religious leader, and an army to back her up," Sam Sloan said. "Now, that's a sweet setup."

"So what the hell do we do about it?" McKay asked.

FitzSimmons raised his eyebrows. "Isn't that obvious? You're supposed to go down there and make sure this *Hermana Luz* doesn't become Queen of Mexico.

"*Dead* sure."

CHAPTER
THREE

"Questioning orders, McKay?" The satellite-relayed voice of Dr. Jacob Morgenstern asked.

McKay hesitated. "Yeah."

A moment, punctuated with the thin crackle of static. Then: "Good. It's part of your job to show initiative." And a laugh, dry as a wind up out of the Chihuahuan desert.

Dr. Jacob Morgenstern, who had helped the mysterious Major Crenna put together Project Blueprint and had now succeeded him in administering it, had done everything once. Things he'd liked he'd done twice. Even some things he hadn't. He'd jumped into Mitla Pass with Sharon and the boys, and commanded a tank brigade in the Golan Heights in '73. He'd told the Japanese where their vaunted management techniques were all wrong, shortly before their economy hit the shoals. He was a master of aikido. After the war he'd trekked up and down the California coast like a lonely pilgrim of commerce, tying survivors into a network of mutual support through trade; during the incursion by the Federated States of Europe he'd used the network as a matrix for resistance. He had his shit as together as anyone McKay had ever known, and that included the late Major Crenna, whom all the Guardians regarded with something akin to worship.

Best of all, he couldn't take Marguerite Connoly either.

"What do you have on your mind, Lieutenant?" Morgenstern asked, in a tone that said he knew.

"I just wanted to get this straight. You want us to go to Mexico City and off a teenage girl?"

"Not necessarily."

McKay looked at the other Guardians, clustered in the gloom of Mobile One with their faces underlit by the glow from the Electronic Systems Operator's console. "You're waffling, Doc. That ain't like you."

"I am speaking with my customary precision, Lieutenant," Morgenstern said tartly. "It is not required that you kill *Hermana Luz*. It's only necessary for you to remove her from the scene."

"That sounds like a shallow grave on the outskirts of town to me, but then I'm only a dead-end kid from Pittsburgh." He took a deep breath. "You're saying you go along with this?"

"With reservations, yes. Mexico is a country in which— what's the word?—*personalismo* is of great importance. This Sister Light is popularly supposed to be in direct communication with the Virgin Mary. If you remove her from the scene—not necessarily by killing her, but however—then you cut the heart out of the *Cristero* movement."

"An appropriate metaphor," Sloan said. "The Aztecs—"

"Don't hit me with metaphors now, Sloan, that's all I need."

"It might work, Billy," Casey said. "That's, like, what happened with the New Dispensation people, after we took out Coffin."

"Yeah, but this is a whole different country . . . fuck it. I'm a marine; you tell me, saddle up and go, I saddle up and go, and that's all there is to it. If this is the way you say to play it, Doc, I'm with you all the way."

"It's not the way I necessarily would have chosen to 'play it,' as you put it. But I see no alternative, given the press of circumstances. Chairman Maximov must not be permitted to gain control of Mexico."

"Fuckin'-A straight."

"I do have to warn you, Lieutenant McKay, that you're going to be operating under constraints not of my choosing. Though

I am nominally responsible for both the Guardians and Project Blueprint, I do not yet enjoy full autonomy."

"Oh, boy," McKay said. "I can't wait."

When he found out what the "constraints" were, he hit the ceiling.

"You want me to take along a whole squad of troopies, four indiges, some Mexican wheel, *and* a cookie pusher from the State Department? What the fuck? Don't you want me to take a marching band with me, too?" He spun around and glared at FitzSimmons. "What if we have to have a goddamned parade?"

Sitting in a cowhide-covered chair beneath a sprawling water-color of the Staked Plains, Dreadlock Callahan grinned and blew smoke from the slim black cigar stuck in his piratical face. He was a long, lean, light-skinned black dressed at the moment in cammies and web gear, which went strangely with the handlebar mustache framing his mouth and the long ropy braids that gave him his nickname. The first time the Guardians had met him he was the leader of a biker gang pressed into service by the Children of the New Dispensation against their will—or so he said.

These days he was at least semirespectable, having attained the rank of major in the armed forces of the Republic of Texas—a mercenary, like Eklund, though unlike Eklund he wasn't a native of the state. At the moment he was playing bearer of bad tidings, and obviously enjoying the role.

"Your people asked us to provide you assistance," Callahan said. "That's why the troopies and the guides. Somebody to wipe your butts and keep you from getting in too much trouble with the locals. The cookie pusher's not our idea, believe me."

"Shit," McKay said. He was pacing the maroon tiles of the office. His three fellow Guardians were sitting on a leather-covered sofa with a black and gray Navajo blanket draped over the back of it, not looking as if they enjoyed what they were hearing much better than he did. Tom Rogers was almost frowning. That in itself was the equivalent of most men hollering and busting up the furniture.

"It's either too many or too damned few," Mckay said. "I mean, if we're gonna invade the country, let's go in with an honest to Jesus army, kick some ass, and take some names.

Otherwise just the four of us are plenty.''

Callahan let smoke trail out of his nostrils. It gave him a Mephistophelean appearance. He wasn't unaware of the fact. "Your boss says different, McKay. He says you need support, which we are politely providing you as allied of the United States of America. Don't sprain anything important leaping to thank us, McKay.''

"There's more," the burly old man behind the desk the size of Deaf Smith county said.

McKay turned to face him, head held low like a bull facing the cape, just managing to hold his temper and his tongue. The old man was even bigger than he was, and the years hadn't noticeably softened him. Besides, in his day he'd done his stint as a combat marine, and left a foot behind at Frozen Chosin in North Korea.

Also, he was president of the Republic of Texas.

"It isn't our idea, either, believe me, son," Lamar Louis Napoleon LaRousse said in a voice like a rock polisher. He sighed like Mount Saint Helens letting one. "I suppose I should let you see for yourself.''

He pressed a button on the fancy telephone next to the Remington cast brass statue of a cowboy busting a bronc on his desk. The door opened and two men and a woman came in.

As a natural matter of course McKay took in the woman first. At first he thought she was another of the president's innumerable ex-wives: taller than any others he'd seen, slender, and just plain beautiful, with an oval olive-skinned face and long gleaming black hair and eyes of a startling jade green. But where the others were all great-looking middle-aged women, this one couldn't be more than seventeen. *You dirty old man!* McKay thought, shocked in spite of himself.

Callahan laughed. "Don't burn your eyes, McKay. It's his daughter.''

The president beamed beneath a mustache no less villainous than Callahan's, and the white of the snow—a rarity before the war messed up climate patterns—melting into the hill country. "Gentlemen, permit me to introduce my youngest, Claudia Marie. Claudia, meet the Guardians: Sam Sloan, Tommy Rogers, Casey Wilson, and this here ornery bronco is Billy

McKay. He offers to show you his longarm, honey, don't you let him."

Claudia dropped her eyes and a pretty dusky pink dusted her cheeks. McKay thought he caught her flicking him a quick glance from beneath her eyebrows, though, as she muttered something about how pleased she was to meet them.

"You git along now, Claudia," LaRousse said. Claudia turned and walked out, erect. Just before she shut the door she caught McKay's eye and winked.

Son of a bitch, he thought. Then: *Whoa, there, my man.* He could envision the president of the Republic of Texas tying a knot in his tallywhacker for even *thinking* those thoughts about his baby girl. He could also imagine the crusty old fuck not giving two hoots in Hell if Mckay humped his downy chick all the way down the Balcones Escarpment. For all that he wore his hair to his shoulders and carried on like a comic book Texan fool, LaRousse was smart, mean, and unpredictable as an old alpha-male timber wolf.

LaRousse waved a hand at the nearer of the two men his daughter had brought in. He was a tall man in a dark suit, with a round smooth face and dark hair and a general air of being pissed off at being ignored during the byplay with Claudia LaRousse.

"This here's Powell Gooding. They flew him down last night from Washington. He's with the State Department; he's going along with you."

"He is, is he?" McKay grunted. He shook Gooding's hand. The grip was strong: racquetball muscle. *What is this, Attack of the Killer Preppies?*

"I'm pleased to meet you, Lieutenant McKay," Gooding said in a voice that was much too smooth. "I've heard a lot about you."

"You have, huh? Just why is it we're supposed to be dragging you along, anyway?"

"To help prevent any untoward incidents that might sour relations with our neighbors to the south."

Sam Sloan laughed sourly. "We're going to assassinate a popular religious leader, and you reckon you're going to keep anybody from being unhappy about it?"

Gooding's young-looking face got a pained expression. For a diplomat he sure didn't have much of a poker face, McKay thought. "Please. This isn't a joking matter. And, please, not 'assassination.' Our mission is to neutralize *Hermana Luz.* That's only one of our options."

Sloan rubbed his jaw and nodded. He looked less than convinced.

The last man in the room stood quietly by with a dove-gray Stetson in his hand. He was average height at best, very spare, with straight sandy-gray hair, a prominent nose with a brush of mustache beneath it. He looked to be in his forties. He was dressed well in a not too emphatically Western way.

"Finally, President LaRousse said, nodding to him, "I'd like to introduce the final member of your party: Captain Samuel Coates of the Texas Rangers."

The Texican squad that was getting sent into Mexico with the Guardians was training at some former elementary school. Next morning Callahan had his second in command and current squeeze, a rangy platinum blonde named Sherri, drive them over in a Blazer. Callahan swore up and down she was a seasoned combat trooper. He may even have been telling the truth.

McKay was sitting in back with his arms folded across his chest, hard at work feeling sorry for himself. He had plenty of reasons. One of them was that Eklund had never come back to her little house last night. He'd wanted to try to make up for the morning's fight—wanting to talk to somebody who understood what life was really like, who knew what it was to have your ass on the line, about the shit-pit he and his buddies had landed in. He'd been tempted to gather up his gear and head back downtown to where the other Guardians were bivouacked, but instead he kept hanging on and hanging on, until he finally said fuck it and fell asleep on her bed with his boots on, drawing satisfaction from the fact that it would piss her off mightily in case she came back and caught him.

Now he was pissed off at her. He wasn't used to sitting up half the night waiting on some bitch, wondering where she was and what she was doing there and who with. That wasn't supposed to happen to him.

Sam hung his face over the back of the front seat. As always he looked early morning fresh, something McKay had never managed to master even as a DI at Parris Island, though there he'd been able to cover up by being such a noxious son of a bitch no boot dared look at him with both eyes at once. Goddamned Sloan had probably run fifty miles by the time McKay groaned his way awake in Eklund's bedroom. Lousy candy-assed navy bastard, always trying to show you up.

"Why aren't you coming along with us, Dreadlock?" Sloan asked. "Everybody else is."

Callahan was gazing out the window at a bunch of kids playing in a playground, swarming all over a wooden contraption that put McKay in mind of a Habitrail for humans. "I'd love to," he said without looking away from the window. "But they tell me I can't be spared. They're expecting things to heat up near the Okie border, now that Randy Jim's set up his government in exile under Forrie Smith's wing. That's my line of country up there. 'Swhere I've spent most of my time since I signed on."

"Listen at him," Sherri drawled derisively. "He's carryin' on like he's Mr. West Point, R.A. Duty calls, and all that shit. And he's just a raggedy-ass merc." Sherri had substantial boobs and a touch of hardness at the corners of her mouth and eyes, and came across like a foulmouthed Texas bimbo—a topless dancer at a bad bar on 66, perhaps. She was allegedly Regular Army herself. She negotiated the mostly clear San Antonio streets with enough wildness to show she knew what she was doing and mostly didn't give a damn.

He hauled himself around, a rare look of irritation on his face. "Well, crap, I can always resign and tag along after the Guardians as a private citizen, and let you take over from me."

"Naw. You'd just catch you a dose from some Meskin sweet-thing and slow everybody else up."

"You could go along with us," Sloan said. McKay kind of looked at him, decided he was just making conversation. Sherri was not Sam's type in spades. He went for willowy women who ate crumbly cheese and drank California wine that wasn't Gallo and knew about opera and gallery openings and shit like that.

"If you really want," Callahan said, "though just between

the two of us, Mexico's full enough of crazy women without you importing any into the country."

"Asshole," Sherri offered.

"The thing is, it'd be a change of policy. As things stand, this is an all-male operation. The way it ought to be."

"Male chauvinist asshole," Sherri amended.

"Right on," McKay said with feeling.

Callahan turned him a hurt look. "I thought you were my friend."

"No, I don't mean you're a male chauvinist asshole. Or, yes, I do—just like me. 'Cause I think it's right on we don't take any women with us on this little safari. We got trouble enough."

. Sherri turned him a poison look, then straightened her head just in time to swerve around a rubble cart made by cutting the bed and hind tires off a junked pickup and hitching them to a horse.

"Why do we have to take this bunch of bozos with us, anyway?" McKay complained. "I'd at least rather pick my own team. We had some pretty good troop with us at the Galves plant. People we know, people we've worked with."

"Well, first of all, it's kind of a diplomatic thing," Callahan explained. "Cementing relations and all. This unit's elite, a source of civic pride. Texans are a simple, bucolic, clannish kind of people. Put great stock in stuff like this."

"Son of a bitch bluebelly," Sherri spat. She sounded a lot like Eklund sometimes.

"Second, neither your people nor ours would let anybody who'd been through the Galves siege go with you anyway."

McKay scowled. "What the fuck, over? Why not? Those people fought damned well—"

"*Too* well." Callahan took out a cigar and studied it. "They're burned out."

"Combat fatigue, Billy," Tom Rogers said.

McKay chewed on that for a bit. Over a period that could run from a few weeks to months, depending on how intense things got, the psychological casualty rate of a unit in combat was as near a hundred percent as made no difference. It was a real thing, Georgie Patton notwithstanding. Troopers got that thousand-meter stare, started to flake out, stop responding, or maybe started flying into tears or violent rage at any provocation. *Le cafard,* they used to call it in the French Foreign Legion. The bug.

. . . That was any unit except the Guardians. Probably the most important trait they'd been selected for, more so even than physical and mental toughness, brilliant combat records, or lack of close family ties, was a total immunity to firing-line stress. Because the Guardians' job was to recover the hidden pieces of the Blueprint for Renewal, and that meant they were always stuck right into it, with no replacements available, no rotation to the rear.

The Guardians had the resiliency to leap straight from the frying pan of the Gulf coast siege into the Mexican fire without twitching out. Hardly anybody else did, no matter how hardcore they were.

So we're freaks, he thought. *Fuck us.*

"We're there," Sherri said.

There was a consistency to public educational buildings, specifically elementary schools, though you could catch it in high schools, too. Even McKay was aware of it, and he didn't give a whole lot of thought to architecture.

Back in Pittsburgh the public elementary school he'd attended before he got shipped off to the tender mercies of the nuns at St. Grobian's had the aloof, sooty-brick traditional look of an Eastern jail of the Civil War era. The school where Special Duty Squad 551 was quartered, on the other hand, was a sprawl of cinder-block boxes painted in wide, hard-edged swatches of these weird off colors: not-rust, not-turquoise, 7-11 mustard. It had a more modern, Territorial Prison look, like an update of something out of a Sergio Leone western: 1954 Ranch-Style Honor Farm. The coils of razor tape looping around the hardpan playground only added to the impression.

The troopies had a regular obstacle course set up on the grounds and were going through their paces below a sky that threatened to break out in patches of blue at any moment. Callahan and the Guardians sauntered over in that direction while Sherri got out, slammed the door, crammed a camouflaged boonie hat down on the tight silver bun she'd tied her hair into, and propped her attractive ass on the Blazer's black hood.

McKay felt familiar stirrings inside at watching the squaddies climbing ropes and hurdling barriers and running through tires, a sense of hearkening back to older, simpler days. Not nostalgia—not for obstacle courses. He was hard-core, not stupid.

One of them finished well ahead of the rest and came to meet them, wiping his hands on his cammie pants. He was blond and clean-shaven, tall as McKay but lighter built, more a quarterback type than linebacker. He moved with the rangy grace of a greyhound, but without the hyper quality.

He stopped a few meters away and snapped off a parade-deck salute. "Howdy," he said, in a moderate West Texas accent. "I'm Sergeant First Class Steve O'Neal. I'm straw boss of this chicken outfit. You must be the Guardians."

He grinned like the sun coming out. "You know, y'all are sort of heroes of mine. Used to read everything I could about you." The way he said it, with a schoolboy's openness, made it not sound hokey at all.

He shook hands all around. At close range good-looking in a way that would have been pretty-boy except for little evidences that he'd been knocked around some—the nose that wasn't quite straight, assorted little nicks and scratches, a feral watchfulness in the blue eyes. Looking at him, McKay could tell he knew first-hand what it was like to have the shit-storm howling around your ears. That was some consolation.

"Lieutenant McKay," he said, and damned if there wasn't a catch in his voice. "It's a special pleasure to meet you. You were sort of a legend in the Corps when I was a boot."

Well, *that* certainly squelched any temptation McKay might have had to play the Crushing Handshake game, even though he was sure he'd win. Well, ninety percent sure. "What, you mean the record I set for getting my ass busted back to E-1?"

O'Neal laughed. "That and other things. Hi, Major Callahan." Callahan slipped up a corner of his mouth and nodded acknowledgement. O'Neal seemed a bit wary of Callahan, which was a mark in his favor in McKay's book. McKay would trust the former biker chieftain with his life anytime, his wallet with reservations, and his sister when they made Hell a skating rink. But for somebody who didn't know Callahan as well to distrust him showed good judgment.

"So what do you think of my boys?" O'Neal asked. They

were all finishing up now, a dozen young men with vigorous good health sort of busting out of them, roughhousing with each other like so many bear cubs and wolf-calling at Sherri, who was reading a Harlequin and ignoring them without effort. They were mostly big and mostly white, though there were exceptions, like the wiry little Hispanic dude who slid down the final rope and then turned a complete flip as he ran over, like Ozzie Smith taking the field at Busch.

To McKay's DI eye they had a strak look to them. "Looking good," he admitted. "But how they look on the obstacle course is only part of it."

"Sure," O'Neal said, nodding. "Sure. This is Sergeant Bill Warner, Corporal Jason Matlock, and Corporal Buck Toliver, my fire-team leaders."

The three shook hands with the Guardians. Matlock was a black about Tommy Rogers' height, with a weightlifter's build, chest just ballooning up out of his trousers, and shoulders as wide as McKay's. He'd bear watching; iron-pumpers frequently didn't have the sort of stamina it took to crawl through a klick of mud with AK bullets cracking overhead. He had an 82nd Airborne patch on his shirt.

Toliver was another beefy blond with a football jock's build and battered face. His voice sounded like bad bearings from cigarettes, cheap tequila, and a few good forearm blocks to the larynx. The globe and anchor tattoo on his right biceps told McKay a few welcome things.

Warner, O'Neal's second, stood a centimeter or so taller than McKay and had the look of being packed in till your skin stretched smooth that you only got if you were a sausage or somebody who took military-style fitness training seriously. He had a brush of stiff dark brown hair and very round blue eyes that seemed to glare out of a heavy face the color of Georgia clay. His tattoo said Rangers—Kill 'Em All, Let God Sort 'Em Out.

"So you're the Guardians," he said when he was introduced.

"We like to think so," Sam said. Warner gave him a look.

"You think you're pretty tough, huh? Tell you what. Let's you and us have a friendly competition, just to get to know each other. Run the course against the clock, just for starters."

The Guardians looked at each other, then three of them

looked at McKay. McKay rolled his big jaw around in his face.

"Not this time," he said slowly.

"Why the hell not? Afraid to get those shiny jumpsuits dirty?" The Guardians had on their silver-gray coveralls this morning.

"Yeah," McKay said. "It costs the taxpayers money to get these things clean. We can't go messin' them up playing games."

Warner's face went redder and his eyes popped out a bit. He was ready to say something more, but O'Neal laughed and interposed himself. "Hey, take it easy. The Guardians have got better things to do than roll around in the dirt this morning. They've got a mission to plan." But you could read the disappointment in his voice.

Driving back, Callahan asked, "Why didn't you take Warner up on it, McKay? You don't actually think those puppies could take you?"

McKay laughed. "Shit no."

Callahan cocked an eyebrow. "You don't think I buy that bullshit about the taxpayers, do you? This is the Dreadlock you're talking to."

"Dreadlock, my man, let me give you the ungarbled word. We are the Guardians. That means we are by definition the best. We do not have to compete to prove it. We just *are*."

Callahan jutted his chin and nodded. "I'll buy that."

But it was Tom who had the last word, as usual. "We're going to have some trouble with those boys," he said.

And Tom was always right.

CHAPTER
FOUR ────────────────────

The girl stood by the balcony gazing out at the vast emptiness of the nighttime city. Here and there oil drum fires in the squatters' camps seemed to float like orange blossoms on a great black lake, deceptively lovely. Somewhere off to the south a building burned, a garish shout against a sky from which the smog had filtered most stars. Otherwise the enormous valley was filled with darkness, disturbed only by vagrant gleams of kerosene light escaping through curtains too carelessly closed to conceal violation of the blackout and curfew that had been in effect since the *Cristero* horde appeared on the city's brink.

Manuel Tejada stepped from the hotel room behind her. He meant to be quiet, but a scattering of fine grit from the volcano crunched beneath the leather sole of his shoe. The girl started, turned halfway.

"Oh. It's only you, Manuel." His heart stumbled slightly at the sight of her, her exquisitely sculpted features turned to a silver mask by diffuse moonlight. "You frightened me."

He put a smile on his puffy moon of a face. He wasn't fat, just heavyset, and a bit bloated in his cream-colored suit. He was tall for a Mexican. He had a huge head, big even for his body, an unhealthy sallow-olive complexion, and a limp mustache. His eyes had sad dark daubs beneath them.

"There's nothing to be afraid of, *Hermanita*. Your faithful surround this place. No evil men could possibly reach you—and don't forget you have the Virgin Herself watching over you."

Out there in the distance a siren began to burble moronically: *bee*-boo, *bee*-boo, cicada song electronically condensed. There were the hollow thumps of gunfire, once, twice, then a flurry of shots like hail on a shanty's cardboard roof. *Hermana Luz* touched a slender hand to the crucifix at her throat.

"The Virgin speaks to me," she whispered absently, and crossed herself. "But I have to bear my own crosses." A final shot punctuated the words.

The long almond-shaped eyes were almost shut. He found his hand raised, almost touching the long black hair that hung unbound down the back of her simple peasant dress. The hair had a bit of kink in it; it wasn't arrow-straight Indian hair. Sister Light was a *mestiza,* part European and part *indigena*— Indian—a true daughter of Mexico.

It was part of the reason she was about to make Manuel Tejada *de facto* ruler of Mexico.

He pulled his hand hastily back. She hadn't noticed the near intimacy, fortunately. Nothing could be allowed to upset her trust in him, the man who had discovered her in the dusty, dry hills along the edge of the Valley of Mexico, who had made her first the wonder of the nation and then, to many, its divinely appointed savior.

Manuel Tejada Riojos thought of himself as a businessman and a selfless public servant. He was wrong on both counts. His experience in "business" had been as an executive of *Petróleos Mexicanos,* the Mexican oil company, which belonged to the Mexican government. Which in turn meant it was a wholly owned subsidiary of the Party of Institutionalized Revolution, PRI, which had run the country from the Revolution until very shortly before the One-Day War. The nationalized oil industry had opened up whole new dimensions of corruption during the American oil crunch of the Seventies, and for nearly twenty years had been the most lucrative siphon the PRI had stuck into the mainstream of the Mexican economy. Tejada had played a small but vital role in sticking the needle in, and had profited accordingly.

His substantial and not altogether licit income had supported a weepy, dumpy, compulsively pious wife, two hopeless sons (one a journalist for a paper run by the government, the other a minor party functionary in Guerrero, the PRI's equivalent of Siberia, only hotter) and two daughters, one of whom had been shunted into a convent and one who had run off with a truck driver from Michoacán. He also contributed heavily to various worthy causes including the Society for the Preservation of the Anáhuac, which hearkened back to the good old pre-Cortez days, when men were men and gods were mean sons of bitches who had to be propitiated with gallons of blood in hopes they'd hold off the monsters who lived beneath the horizon and were *really* nasty. He had also maintained a string of leggy mistresses who shared a taste for apartments in the *Zona Rosa* and your pricier signature exports of Paris and Colombia.

With the collapse of PRI and their rivals, PAN, and the rise of the coalition which had brought Enrique Córdoba to power, Tejada had found himself out of a job. He'd kept the mistresses in coke and designer dresses and the wife in candles to burn to assorted saints by hiring squatters to go and sit in peasants' fields. Since redistribution of the land was an institutionalized goal of the Mexican government, sooner or later their claims would be recognized and deeds issued them—which they would, as agreed in advance, surrender to Tejada for a fraction of their worth.

It had been on a tour of prospective acquisitions in desolate San Luis Potosí that he had discovered Sister Light preaching in a derelict beanfield. His first thought on seeing her was that she was the most beautiful girl he'd ever set eyes on. Then he saw the rapt expressions on the faces of the farmers and dirt-poor laborers listening to her, and his PRI-honed instinct for the main chance kicked in, overriding thoughts of romance.

Now—tonight—he had to keep those thoughts overriden. *Hermana Luz* was, after all, the country's most prominent living virgin. It wouldn't do to risk sullying her reputation—not to mention what her fanatical followers, who would hurl themselves against machine-gun emplacements in her name, would do to anyone they so much as suspected of impure thoughts about her.

He made himself step back. "Come, *Hermana*, let your attendants put you to bed. Tomorrow I go to consult with those fools of ministers at the palace again. God may will that you make your triumphal entry tomorrow."

She frowned, gestured at the flame-flecked night. "There are those who resist my entry."

"Bah. Heretics and fools, whose lust for power blinds them to your radiance. They'll come around."

"No." she shook her head. "Not them. The common people . . . they don't yet accept me."

"Then their disbelief will be their destruction." His words rang out so stridently that heads turned in the little park across the street, where *Cristeros* patrolled the trees with Soviet automatic weapons, the gifts of Sister Light's most influential admirer. "Your faithful shall strike them down in their apostasy."

She looked down at her hands. Tejada snapped his fingers, and two aged Indian women emerged from the candle-lit room behind them to lead the prophetess to bed.

Tejada watched her go with exultation bubbling around inside him. Soon she would rule all Mexico—and through her, *he* would rule. When that happened, it would no longer be so vital to guard Sister Light's virginity. Only its appearance.

Of course, just as he stood invisibly behind *Hermana Luz*, another stood invisibly behind him, pulling his strings. He would be ruling Mexico as viceroy of Yevgeny Maximov, Chairman of the Federated States of Europe. As a patriot, the thought filled him with indignation.

Someday, he told himself, turning to gaze out into the great bowlful of night, that held what was still one of the world's largest cities. He wasn't fool enough to imagine he could have come this far without the aid of Maximov's henchman, that supple pale devil who called himself Ian Victor. But his status as a puppet rankled him.

At least he was an indispensible puppet. With its chronic distrust of outside intervention, the vast paranoid beast of the Mexican public would never tolerate a foreigner in *Hermana Luz's* inner council. Maximov and "Ian Victor" *needed* him.

Otherwise he didn't doubt for an instant that Victor would long since have liquidated him as facilely as he had eliminated that odious communist Orozco.

The thought of the MAR leader's murder tightened fleshy lips beneath his damp mustache. Necessary as it was—laudable, even—that assassination had shown him the writing on the wall. Should Maximov or his lethal lapdog so much as suspect him of thoughts of double-dealing, they'd put him out of the way in spite of everything, and try to find some more pliant local to manipulate Sister Light. So he would keep his resentments and his hopes in a very distant, private corner of his mind.

Somewhere a tape machine began to play a song in the *Huastec* style, all steel harp and harsh nasal chanting. Maximov and Victor would learn the lesson of Mexico soon enough. The lesson learned by the Spanish, and the French, and the Americans—even by the Toltecs and later the Aztecs themselves, who came down from the north as barbarian conquerors, only to fall before invaders in their turn: that alien intruders were either absorbed or gave up and went home.

And that Mexico endured.

"Vera Cruz," Billy McKay said, and belched Pearl beer. "Sonofabitch."

"Yeah," Sam Sloan agreed. He was perched on the edge of a picnic table set out on San Antonio's Military Plaza beside City Hall. The light of bonfires and barbecue pits jury-rigged from fire brick danced in the darkened windows of the skyscraper, which had lost its upper stories to the One-Day War. He had a Texas-sized tumbler of whiskey in his hand. Following his commander's lead, he was setting out to do something most uncharacteristic of him: get blind drunk.

Off on the bricks of the Plaza a costumed band was playing *mariachi* music. Steam gouted from the trumpets like the smokestacks of McKay's Pittsburgh youth as they blatted out a fanfare. It was still getting chilly down here at night, another leftover of the war. A global thermonuclear exchange hadn't brought a "nuclear winter," but it had dislocated the climate in a lot of weird ways.

Tom Rogers wandered their way from talking to four skinny

norteños, northern Mexican farmers in sheepskin jackets who'd been pushed off their land by the *Cristeros* and would guide the Guardians and their expeditionary force south day after tomorrow. He had a can of beer in his hand. That was all Billy McKay had ever seen him drink at one time, in all the years they'd been a team: one single, solitary beer.

"They ain't too happy about things, either," the former Green Beret remarked. He spoke good, rough and ready Spanish, though with a more southerly accent than their guides-to-be were used to. Still, he had a way of making himself understood. After all, he'd at one time been the Ultimate Green Beanie, saboteur, infiltrator, and cadreman extraordinaire, just as McKay was the Maximum Marine.

A shift in the wind brought the aroma of burning mesquite and meat curling up their noses like tentacles. The Republic of Texas was giving them a good old-fashioned down home Texas barbecue as a sendoff. The fact that it was still the goddam winter just didn't slow them down one bit. These Texicans knew how to party hearty.

"A thousand miles to Mexico fucking City," Billy McKay said with slurred anger. A straight shot south from San Antone actually ran a thousand kilometers, somewhere over six hundred miles. But the westward jog into Chihuahua, to avoid traveling through an estimated hundred thousand *Cristero* remaining in Coahuila and Nuevo León, north of *Hermana Luz's* home state of San Luis Potosí, ran the total up another four hundred miles.

"We could sail down to Vera Cruz in comfort, and then have a mere two hundred klicks overland to Mexico City. But *nooooo.*" He did his bitter best John Belushi. "We have to shag ass through a thousand miles of sand, scorpions, and hostile indiges."

Sam hoisted his glass. "All when we could cruise down in comfort." He swayed a little. *Whoa,* he thought, *I have to remember I don't have much practice at this.*

"Why so glum, boys?" It was Captain Coates of the Texas Rangers, with his own tumbler of whiskey in hand.

Blinking at him, McKay noticed the hair at the sides of his head was a touch redder than that on top, which was blond and longish. *Son of a bitch's wearing a toupee,* he guessed. *Jesus. All we need.*

The band had started in on a *mariachi* arrangement of Beethoven's Fifth Symphony, which was maybe the one piece of classical music McKay could recognize, even if *this* was done to it. "Nothin' much," McKay said, not trying to sound a lot less hostile than he felt. "Just us invading Mexico with a whole mob of people along a route that means we're liable to have to fight our way all the way to Mexico City."

Coates chuckled. "Ain't half that bad, son. We've got Colonel Gutiérrez meeting us in Chihuahua. He's a straight dude. Used to work with him a lot, catching drug runners before the war, he was in real heavy with the DEA. His troops'll escort us straight to the Federal District, no sweat."

McKay grunted.

Coates got a cagey look in his eye. "Somethin' else eating you boys?" he asked.

Sam Sloan started to shake his head, reflexively polite. So McKay of course blurted, "Yeah. Why the hell are you down here instead of up in Oklahoma City with your main man Randy Jim?"

CHAPTER
FIVE

"McKay—" Sloan started in exasperation. The Ranger shook his head slowly.

"There's been a bad misunderstanding. Governor Hedison maybe made a few bad judgment calls, and now he's paying the price. I don't doubt he'll clear his name as soon as things settle down a tad, I don't doubt it for a minute."

He looked McKay square in the eye. "As for why I'm down here, son, I'm a loyal American doing my duty. Not like some people I could name." He nodded his head generally at the mass of Texicans. "I'm here to show that the State of Texas is still proud to be part of the United States of America."

"Yeah," McKay grunted again. He hated the idea of secession. But the secessionist Texicans had made themselves comrades in arms, while the Federal Texans—the Rangers in particular—had made themselves enemies. He couldn't quite bring himself to trust the trim little captain.

"I'm sure it'll be a pleasure working with you, Captain Coates," Sam Sloan said, slurring his words slightly.

"Call me Sudden Sam, son. All my friends do." He grinned suddenly. "Help us know which one of us somebody wants when they call out 'Sam.' Save one of us havin' to be known as 'Hey, you,' " He slapped Sloan on the arm. "C'mon, I'll introduce you boys to Severino. Our contact man with the government of Chihuahua."

To most Mexicans, the *norteños* of the northern states were known for their toughness and independence. The rest of the country thought they were too close to the *norteamericanos,* with whom they had a love-hate relationship going back to the 1842 war, but at the same time romanticized them as hard-nosed *vaquero* hellraisers, real men's men, real Mexicans; most of the better-known leaders of the Revolution had been *norteños,* from Obregón to Pancho Villa. They were also suspected of impiety; the northern ranchers had suffered enormously under the invading *Cristero* fanatics.

Severino López was an assistant to the governor of the State of Chihuahua who had been serving as liaison to the Republic since the *Cristero* crisis began. He was a tall, slender, worried-looking man with the almost obligatory Zapata sweep of mustache and graying hair. He stood conversing with President LaRousse, who was affecting snow-white fringed buckskins for the night's celebration.

"Enjoying the victory bash, gentlemen?" LaRousse asked the Guardians, with a hoist of his own tumbler and a conspiratorial wink. The barbecue was ostensibly to commemorate the victory at the Galves plant, to cover its real purpose of being the send-off for the Mexico City expedition, which was supposed to be a secret. Every last one of the several hundred celebrants busy hogging down the ribs, sucking up booze, and dancing on the Plaza knew perfectly well what was going on. Security was not a Texican strong suit.

"Uh, yeah," McKay said. "It's great."

Nodding politely to Coates, LaRousse introduced the three Guardians to López. "It's a very great thing you are doing," the Chihuahuan said gravely as he shook McKay's hand, "helping rescue my country from these fanatics."

"Any time," McKay said.

He felt Sloan giving him the fish eye and decided it was time for some chow. He mumbled an excuse and wandered off in the direction of the hot tables.

He had just loaded a scarfed plastic plate with a ton of beans, greens, corn bread, and charred ribs dripping maroon sauce when a bright young voice said, "Hi, there," behind him.

He turned. It was Claudia LaRousse in a frilly blouse and blue jeans, with her long black hair pulled back in a ponytail. The blouse was cut low enough to emphasize the line of demarcation dividing an impressive set of breasts.

"Uh, hi," he said, spilling corn bread crumbs from his mouth and looking wildly around to see if the piercing blue presidential eye happened to be turned his way, while trying not to be obvious about it. He'd only had a pair of six packs, which wasn't enough to make him think he was succeeding.

"I know you're about ready to set off on your big secret mission," the girl said, eyes gleaming like emeralds in the bonfire light. She had her voice dropped low and conspiratorial. It rasped right along McKay's scrotum. *Down, boy,* he thought.

"I just wanted to say goodbye and give you something for good luck," she said.

"Well, shi—I mean, that's real nice of you, Claudia—"

She hooked him around the neck with surprisingly strong arms and yanked his head down for a kiss. Her mouth was open. Her tongue was active. Agile, too.

"There," she said when she broke away. She dropped her eyes, blinked amazingly long black lashes, and then McKay was damned if she didn't blush. "I hope that keeps you safe." And then she turned and scampered into the crowd.

Shaking his head, McKay lumbered back toward Sam and Tom. Casey had joined them. He had a beer in his hand. That didn't strike Mckay as a good sign; he'd maybe seen Casey drink anything alcoholic about three times in his life.

Before he reached their redwood table on the outskirts of the happy crowd, which was now dancing to some offkey *mariachi* tune that sounded for all the world to him like the polkas his Polack grandma always used to have on the ancient Motorola when he came to visit, he sensed somebody falling into step with him. He did a quick eyes-right, and almost dropped his overloaded plate.

"Eklund?"

"I see your eyes are still sharp, Yankee boy."

"But you—you're wearing a *dress*."

She swung in front of him and stopped. They were away

from the mob, beneath an unhappy-looking pecan tree sprouting from a square hole in the flagstones. "I'm a girl, in case you didn't notice. We do that sometimes."

"Well, uh." He stared. What she had on was blue and white and seemed to have petticoats puffing out the full skirt. It was cut even lower than little Claudia LaRousse's blouse, and her frontage was even more impressive. She wore high heels, and was looking him square in the eye.

"I'll be damned," he finally got out.

"Been tellin' you that all along."

"But you was a *drill sergeant,*" he sputtered, torn between outrage and lust.

"So? I bet you've known DIs wore dresses before. Heard some mighty peculiar stories about you gyrenes."

McKay felt his face burn. He was preparing to explode all over her like a *fougasse* barrel when she giggled and touched him on the nose.

"I love it when you get pissed off," she said. "You turn all red and swell up like a stepped-on toad-frog."

The air blew out of him in a long "Jesus." He shook his head. "What am I going to do with you?"

"You could kiss me."

He did, making a thorough job of it, now that he didn't have to worry about the president coming after him with a twelve-gauge.

"So where the hell were you?" he growled when they broke apart.

"Round and about. You mean to say you care?"

Frowning silence.

She laughed again, more quietly, and hugged him. Her embrace was as strong as most men's, and he recalled in a beer-bleary way how glad he was she'd grown her hair out. When she had it cropped close he used to get the uncomfortable feeling he was fucking a guy sometimes when they got it on. Nothing going to take the starch out of you quicker than that.

"How come we can't get along?" she asked his pecs.

"How the hell do I know?" He held on to her hard biceps uncomfortably. This kind of talk always made him uneasy.

"Maybe 'cause we love each other," she said. He didn't have anything to say to that. He felt a dry heat prickling in his chest.

He wished she'd change the subject.

"I don't know why I blew off at you like that, the other morning," she said. "All over nothing."

"Hey, it don't mean nothing. Figured you was probably on the rag."

She snapped away from him as if she were hooked to one of those harnesses they use in the movies to make you look as if you've been shot, or at least the way moviemakers think you look when you suck one. "Just what the hell do you mean by that?"

"Well, I mean, sometimes a woman's chemistry gets screwed up, she don't think quite right, you know?"

"You male chauvinist son of a bitch."

He blinked at her. Maybe he should have laid off the whiskey along with all that beer. The edge was off his brain. Here he was trying to be reasonable, allow for her little feminine foibles, and she was climbing down his throat.

"Wha'd I say?" he demanded.

"I saw you necking with that teenybopper, McKay."

"What the fuck, over?"

"You think you can put something over on me. Well, let me tell you something, mister, that black-haired little chit's covered more ground than a flash flood. You needn't go thinking you're big stud on this farm." She turned and stomped off. She wobbled a few steps, apparently unaccustomed to heels, halted and kicked her shoes off, then stalked on without even looking where they fell.

"Shit," McKay said.

He started back to his buddies again. Between Claudia and Marla Eklund, he was working on a fine case of lover's balls tonight. What the hell else could go wrong?

"Yo, McKay," a newly familiar and already unwelcome voice called. "Give us a hand here. Unless you reckon you're too important to talk to us peons."

The 551st Special Duty Squad was clustered around a pickup with its tailgate down and a couple of kegs of beer nestled in a bed of ice, a precious post-Holocaust commodity even in the relatively prosperous Republic of Texas. Sergeant Bill Warner stood in the bed in ice to the tops of his combat boots with the sleeves of his cammies rolled up and a cigarette stuck in his face.

Steve O'Neal met McKay with a hard handshake and a Pepsodent smile. "Good to see you, McKay. Don't mind him; he's just fooling around."

The ex-Ranger's unfriendly smirk belied his words. The other squaddies gathered around affably enough. Sitting on the lowered tailgate of the pickup, Corporal Buck Toliver raised a can of Pearl in salute to McKay. McKay nodded to a lanky towhead named Shiloh and a chunky Nip everyone called Shig and Richard Gallegos, a small and wiry Hispanic from New Mexico who had a faded red can of Tab in his hand. McKay grimaced; if Gallegos could actually drink that shit he was harder-core than McKay ever hoped to be.

'So what can I do for you, Warner?" McKay asked, stopping right behind the truck.

"You can help me unload this mother, Mr. Guardian." He stooped, picked up a keg with the muscles surging in his sunburned arms, and tossed it right at McKay's head.

If he'd been altogether sober McKay probably would have dodged. Instead, without even thinking about it, he put up his right hand, palm up, and caught the keg.

He juggled it for a moment. It felt as if his own biceps was about to pop like an overinflated tire. By some miracle he held it, balanced there on his upturned hand.

The squaddies were watching him with open mouths. Still running on beer-augmented instinct he whipped his big-bladed Kabar knife from its sheath and jammed it up through the thin metal into the keg. He twisted the blade. A frothing amber stream shot out. He grunted and lifted the keg up above his head one-handed, with the muscle in his shoulder creaking like an old door, stuck his face into the stream and drank. Then he tossed the punctured keg to Toliver, who barely managed to field it with both hands.

"Shit, you had you enough," called Tandy, a powerful black troopie. "You done pissed yourself, Buck."

McKay wiped his mouth with the back of his hand. "Thanks for the drink," he said. "Catch you boys later."

"Having a good evening, McKay?" Sam Sloan asked from his picnic table. "Heck, you must be. You smell like a Skid Row mission."

"I love you, too, Navy boy," McKay said.

Casey sat crosslegged on the bricks with his own beer held in both hands, staring at it as though meditating on it. "This isn't going to be very easy, is it, Billy?" he asked quietly, without looking up.

"Aw, shit, Case. It's gonna be a piece of cake. A piece of fucking"—he belched—"cake."

Tom Rogers tipped his bottle to his mouth. "I think maybe I'll have me another."

The others stared at him in horror. Sam almost fell off the table. Tom having a second beer was like a regular human being going on a two-week bender.

"Fuck *us*," McKay said.

"It shall be done," Sam Sloan predicted woefully.

Sometime later, when the chill started to come up out of the bricks and the party started to erode, McKay staggered off to find some relief for his much-abused bladder. The several chemical johns President LaRousse had thoughtfully ordered placed on the Plaza were currently the most popular locales among the partyin' crowd, so McKay went off in search of a field-expedient pisser.

The bushes along the adobe wall of the old Spanish governor's palace across the street drew his attention. He sort of liked that long-haired old bag of wind LaRousse, but the idea of taking a whiz on the presidential residence appealed to him, at least in his present state. He had just unlimbered that which he had taught countless boots was the only item of personal equipment properly describable as a "gun," when he heard voices from around the corner.

Something about him made him sidle to the end of the wall and peer cautiously around. He was just in time to see Marla Eklund loop her arms around the neck of Sergeant First Class Steve O'Neal and kiss him on the mouth. Blatant fraternization.

He pulled his head back in and discovered that he'd peed all over his boots. The expedition to Mexico was getting off to a hell of a start.

CHAPTER
SIX

Leading a pair of deuce-and-half trucks, the ancient green Carryall jounced down what a couple of years of neglect and gully-washers had left of a two-lane Mexican blacktop highway. The decaying road wound its gradual way among tawny hills and mesas capped with ramparts of hard red sandstone. Away to the right the broken land humped up into a frozen purple wave, the Sierra Madre Occidental, part of the bifurcate backbone of the New World. This country was covered with clumps of grass like grey Brillo pads and spiky vegetation of one kind or another, not including green, and in general depressing as hell. At least to Billy McKay.

On the Carryall's second seat, McKay sat next to the man from Washington and hoped the dynamite-happy *Cristeros* hadn't figured out a way to mine this washboard. If they managed to pop the lead vehicle of this little convoy, the entire leadership of what Sam Sloan insisted on calling the American Expeditionary Force was going to be gone with the wind.

Aside from McKay and Powell Gooding, you had a flattopped blond trooper named Jimmy Jack Roebuck at the wheel, and next to him Severino López of the Chihuahuan government in a white linen Sidney Greenstreet suit, and on the other side of Gooding, Steve O'Neal his own handsome self. In the rearmost seat were Sudden Sam Coates, Corporal Matlock, and another squaddie. Stacked in the back atop assorted gear was lanky blond Shiloh, the machine-gunner for Matlock's Fire Team Charlie. It was what you called cozy.

McKay had given up sweating it. López had insisted on riding in the point vehicle for honor's sake. Gooding needed to be along to babysit him, and McKay had signed for both of them, so he was damned if he'd let either out of his sight. For all his hero-worship of McKay—which in two days' travel had proven to be embarrassingly genuine—O'Neal certainly wasn't going to play tail-end Charlie while the head Guardian escorted the celebrities. They couldn't leave Captain Sudden Sam out without offending the allegedly loyal State of Texas. And of course the well-ripped Corporal Matlock and his boys had to be along to pull security and drive the beast.

Besides, there was officially no danger. They were nearing the rendezvous with Colonel Gutiérrez. Nothing could possibly go wrong.

Gooding was all decked out in a tan suit appropriate for meeting *Coronel* Gutiérrez in—as formal as possible, given that the khaki landscape was inevitably going to get all over the diplomat, and would show up on a darker outfit. He was conversing in Spanish with Señor López. McKay didn't have much of the language himself—an introduction to conversational Spanish had been part of Guardians training, but he'd promptly forgotten most of it, along with everything remotely concerned with computers. Still, it seemed that Gooding was having trouble getting a grasp on the Mexican's colloquial speech. *What the fuck, over?* He thought diplomats were supposed to be able to talk to people.

Ah, well. He told himself it didn't matter. With any luck Gooding wouldn't have to do any talking. They'd blitz into Mexico City, put the touch on Sister Moonshine or whatever the hell she called herself, and blow on out of there.

Yeah. I believe in the Easter Bunny, too.

A stiff wind buffeted the vehicle on its uncertain springs. A good hard gust would whistle through the hardened rubber seals of the windows and move right inside his cammie coveralls with him. It was *cold*. That was wrong; this was desert, and McKay knew deserts weren't supposed to get cold. Actually, from his time in the Mideast and Iran, he knew deserts could get cold as hell, but he didn't let that keep him from feeling the chill was symbolic of how fucked up this whole thing was.

When he got bored with listening to Gooding failing to have an intelligible conversation with López and Sudden Sam's gloomy reminiscences about Vietnam, he could always crank up the volume on his communicator. On his instructions the other Guardians had turned up the gain on the microphones taped to their larynxes, so they'd pick up the general chatter in the other two vehicles as well as what the Guardians said aloud or subvocalized.

"Isn't that a communist group?" he heard Bill Warner ask. Warner was ragging on Casey about his Grateful Dead tour cap, that had that logo with the skull wearing the old Tom Jefferson type wig. Casey had the greatest collection of rock tour caps in the known universe. God knew where he kept them. McKay wasn't sure he'd ever seen Case wear the same one twice. "They were a bunch of stinking commies, right?"

"Hey, man," Casey said, sounding aggrieved. "They were just a band."

"I heard they protested us being in Central America," Warner said. As it turned out, he wasn't as young as he looked. O'Neal wasn't, either; they were both in their late twenties, and had served in Latin America at the same time, though without meeting. "When I was down there, I heard them and a bunch of other commies wrote songs protesting us being there."

"I thought what we were fighting about was so people could, like, say what they wanted to, man." McKay raised his eyebrows; Casey was normally as apolitical as you could possibly be. He was patriotic, that went without saying. But he seldom got down to specifics.

"Talking about fighting, what'd you ever do? I had twenty confirmed kills down in Salvador. And they was just the ones big enough not to toss back. How the hell many kills you ever get?"

"Seven."

"Seven?" McKay heard Warner bray a laugh through his nose. "Seven. What's that? Jack shit."

"He means airplanes," Sam Sloan said. Sloan was riding with Casey, a pair of the guides—who'd gotten bumped from the lead vehicle on account of space limitations, which just figured—and Fire Team Alpha in the third truck. "As in MiGs. As in five shot down in one mission."

"Yeah, I remember that, Bill," said Jaworcki, Alpha's M79 man. "Don't you read the papers? He was a big hero, over in Syria."

"Air Force, huh? Big deal." But the former Ranger sounded less certain.

McKay saw O'Neal hanging his blond head back to talk behind Gooding's neck and dialed down the volume to the bone-conduction speaker taped behind his ear.

"So what do we do with this *Hermana Luz* once we get to her?" O'Neal asked, his poster boy forehead wrinkled with concern.

Shiloh sat up in back and drew his forefinger across his throat. "Cap her. Do her. She's the one started all this."

"Hey, now," said DeWayne Burdick, the other trooper, squeezed in next to Coates and Matlock. "We can't be doing that."

Matlock sat quietly. He had very dark skin with a shiny look, as if he'd been polished in a rock tumbler. He had less to say than even Tom Rogers, which was a mark in his favor where McKay was concerned. Too often muscle boys were the talkative type, always "on," always grabbing for attention. Matlock was shaping up to be as solid as his build.

"You don't think she's killed a mess of women and children?" Shiloh demanded. "You seen what them *Cristeros*'ve done. She don't deserve no better."

Burdick frowned. He didn't have anything to say to that.

"I'm not really sure how responsible she is," O'Neal said. "Our reports say this Manuel Tejada who's fronting her runs a lot of the show. I think she may be one of these types who doesn't have much connection to the real world."

"One way or another," McKay said, "we got to take her down."

O'Neal shook his head sorrowfully. "I understand. It's just that I hope we don't have to hurt her, you know? Maybe it's just wishful thinking, but I don't see her as directly to blame for all the killing being done in her name."

"Spoken like a true Southern gentlemen," Sudden Sam said, only half ironically.

"It is just wishful thinking," McKay affirmed.

O'Neal shrugged. "Our Lord Jesus Christ's had a lot of killing done in His name, too, come to think of it. I only hope we don't have to hurt her."

"Dream on," McKay said. He saw the younger man's face fall. Well, shit. He wanted to hurt his feelings, after that scene with him and Eklund, and yet he didn't. He actually felt a certain amount of jealousy, and that was what pissed him off, that Eklund had that power over him. Try as he might, he couldn't get a good head of anger built up against O'Neal. The kid was too sincere—and thought too highly of him.

"You should've been a Green Beanie like Tommy," he said, softening his earlier words as best he could. "They're always trying to save the world, too."

O'Neal laughed. He seemed flattered by the comparison to Rogers.

They passed a bullet-holed green sign announcing a turnoff for a place called Moctezuma. It seemed to apply to a ribbon of dirt road trailing off in the general direction of nowhere.

"What the hell's a Moctezuma?" McKay wanted to know.

"It is the name of the Aztec First Speaker imprisoned by Cortez," López said in his rich radio announcer's voice. "The man you often call Montezuma."

"You trying to tell me the Corps hymn should go, 'From the Halls of *Moc*tezume?' " McKay asked incredulously. "Jesus. What's the world coming to?"

"You been to the Shores of Tripoli, Billy," Tom Rogers's voice said in McKay's ear, broadcast from the middle vehicle where he was riding with Toliver and Fire Team Bravo. "Now you can say you've come full circle."

"Yeah. I guess I can, at that."

Captain Coates leaned forward. "Start slowing up, son," he told Jimmy Jack. "Just over this hill's where we're meeting Eloy and his people."

"Hold on, hold on," McKay said. Things were stirring around in the back of his brain, like dinosaurs in some prehistoric swamp, or maybe creatures in the bayou country where the Guardians had fought the Effsees alongside a bunch of crazy Cajuns. "Tom, Sam, have 'em stop your vehicles for a moment. Roebuck, you hold it here, too."

He caught the troopie's reflexive glance at the rearview for O'Neal's nod of approval, saw the sergeant's mouth tighten in annoyance; McKay was head of this show, and his orders were supposed to be obeyed without hesitation. *Shit, how can I dislike the dude?* Mckay thought. *He's ready to go all the way for me, even though this outfit's as much his personal property as his toothbrush.*

The convoy came to a halt. "Casey, Sloan, Tom, deass those trucks and spread out to cover. I want some backup."

"Paranoid, McKay?" Sloan asked.

"Shit, yes."

O'Neal had a spare communicator so he could keep in direct touch with the Guardians. He blinked at McKay. "What's the matter?" he asked, genuinely puzzled. "These are the good guys."

McKay looked at him. There was the difference between them. O'Neal had enough combat decorations to make a quilt from, according to Texican military scuttlebutt. But he was a grunt, a line marine, a regular rifleman. McKay had been there, but he'd also played commando with Force RECON and shadow-boxed with the so-called Studies and Observations Group, Southwest Asia Command, the dirty-welfare specialists of the Mediterranean Theater.

Coates chuckled. "He's young, McKay. But still, you're making too much of this. We ain't gonna have no problem."

Gooding looked around like a fresh-hatched chick. "What's going on? What are you talking about?"

"Nothing," McKay said. "Just taking a few precautionary measures."

"I won't have you doing anything that might prejudice our meeting with Colonel Gutiérrez."

"I wouldn't dream of it."

He held them there a few moments to allow the other three Guardians time to spread out and work their way forward, then ordered the convoy into motion.

The breath just sort of unreeled from him as they crested the hill. There was a long, shallow dip maybe five hundred meters from rim to rim, with the road running straight through the center of it. In the exact center was parked a big open four wheeler Ford painted in cammo colors and bristling with antennas. A couple of troopies in camouflaged utilities and old-fashioned steel pot-style American helmets lounged around it, smoking and joking.

Sudden Sam was sucking on a cigarette he'd rolled himself out of a pouch. "See?" he said. "There they are. Everything's smooth as a baby's behind."

"I must say it's a relief to see them there as planned," Gooding said in one of those Ivy League voices that sound as if most of your attention is concentrated on keeping your asshole tight so you won't fart in company. "After the privations of the last two days, I'd begun to acquire rather a fatalistic outlook."

McKay gave him an *Is this guy real?* look. The "privations" of their trip had consisted of riding west into southern New Mexico and camping out at night inside a circle of Claymores, chowing down big time off the mountain of supplies they were trucking along. It was more a camping trip than a sortie. Boy Scout stuff. He caught O'Neal's eye behind Gooding's head and they shared a big old grin.

He couldn't get over a cold feeling, though. It felt as if his stomach were lined in ice. He kept thinking, *I'm leading my team into that?* and telling himself, *Hey, it's cool. This was set up at the highest level. These are the good guys. They're here to help us.*

The Mexican soldiers watched without curiosity as they approached. Roebuck braked to a stop ten or twenty meters away from the command car. A tall man in pressed cammies and a black beret flicked away a cigarette and climbed out to meet them, swinging forward in spit-shined combat boots.

Señor López and Gooding got out first, followed by O'Neal and McKay, who were jostling for priority in a marked but friendly way. "*Buenas dias*," Colonel Guitérrez said. "Welcome to Mexico." His voice was rich, his English heavily accented but clear. He performed a warm *abrazo* with Severino López, then shook hands in a more restrained way with Powell

Gooding, who looked relieved that he wasn't going to get hugged.

He shook hands crisply with O'Neal and McKay. He had a hard look about him, and seemed to be making his way into middle age without carrying a visible gut along. His teeth were very white and even beneath a restrained mustache and a pair of those fancy shades that seem to be covered in a film of oil and block out everything. "I am pleased that you made it here safely, gentlemen. What you are doing is most momentous for my country as well as your own."

"We hope to be of service, Colonel," Gooding said, pitching his voice to carry over the wind that was plucking at his coattails and the blousing of Gutiérrez's trousers. "It's an honor to be here."

Gutiérrez gave him a perfunctory smile and nod. A couple of 551st squaddies deassed the second truck, and a pair of indige guides as well. Gutiérrez ignored them as they wandered up, curious and glad for a chance to stretch their legs.

Then the colonel caught sight of Coates coming out of the Carryall. "Sooden Sam!" he exclaimed, and ran to embrace the Ranger with a volley of rapidfire Spanish.

He pulled back and smoothed down the front of his blouse. "I beg your pardon, gentlemen. It is just that *Capitán* Coates and I are old comrades-in-arms in the war against the *traficantes.*"

"Hey, it's cool," McKay said. "Don't think nothing of it." Coates was grinning at him, like, *I told you so,* and Gooding looked pleased and O'Neal was beaming, happy that it was all working out. The good feelings were so thick you needed a machete to cut through them.

"My troops are bivouacked a few kilometers from here," the Colonel said. "If you would do the honor of following me, I will escort you there so that we may plan our operation."

He turned and started to walk back to his vehicle. A few meters away he stopped and turned back. "But I forget myself. I meet the illustrious Lieutenant McKay and neglect to encounter his equally illustrious comrades. Your fellow Guardians accompany you, do they not?"

Giving McKay a surly sidelong glance, Gooding opened his mouth, saying, "As a matter of fact—"

One of the *norteño* guides, a little dark dude who was mostly sweeping mustache and swordblade nose and was dressed in rough white clothes that looked like nothing so much as a karate *gi,* stepped right in behind the diplomat. "A word, señor, and I cut you," he hissed in Gooding's ear.

The warning was soft, much quieter than the rush and whistle of the desert wind. If McKay hadn't been standing about two meters from Gooding he never would have caught it. He flicked his eye down to see a slim dagger gripped in a hard brown hand, pressing tan fabric above the State Department man's best kidneys.

Gooding froze. The little Mexican's eyes met McKay's.

"Uh, yeah, Colonel," McKay said. "They're back in the trucks." He waved a hand vaguely. "They're looking forward to meeting you, but there'll be plenty of time for that at your camp. Right now, I think what we're all mostly interested in is getting where we're going so we can shower, shave, and shit, and all like that."

Gutiérrez showed a thousand bucks of dental work in a grin. "I sympathize, Lieutenant. I shall endeavor to see your journey ends as soon as possible." He tipped a one-finger salute off his eyebrow and strode to his car.

Powell Gooding watched him go with his mouth working silently like a carp's and a pink flush spreading up his neck. When the colonel had gotten out of earshot, the *norteño* behind Gooding put his knife away and stood back with his hands displayed empty at his sides, submitting himself to the *gringos'* judgment.

Up on the hill behind them, Casey Wilson scanned the ridgeline opposite from the concealment of a broad-blade *mezcal* plant near the road. Through the fancy glass optics of his scope his fighter-pilot's eye caught a hint of something that made him frown. He kicked in the computerized sighting system. The picture shifted slightly as the magnified direct image was replaced by a projected digitalized one. His thumb moved to change the red filtering.

An image sprang out at him.

"Billy," he whispered urgently, "there's people dug in up there. They're sighted right in on you!"

CHAPTER
SEVEN

"I demand that you arrest this man at once," Powell Gooding said, voice trembling with outrage. "I've never been man-handled so outrageously in my life!"

"It's a trap!" McKay screamed, throwing himself at the diplomat in a flying tackle.

Without looking back Gutiérrez jumped into his car while his troopies scrambled aboard. The Ford fishtailed, sending up a shower of stones from the shoulder, and then burned rubber along the cracked asphalt.

Belatedly aware of some of the byplay that had gone on behind his back, Severino López had turned to stare at Gooding and McKay with a puzzled expression. His brown eyes grew wider when he saw the marine hurtling down on top of the diplomat in a cloud of gray dust by the side of the road.

Then his eyes got wider still. A pencil-thick stream of blood spurted from the side of his neck, spattering the road five meters away. He slapped a hand to his neck as though smashing a mosquito. Blood spattered his face and his immaculate suit, but the pulsing didn't slow.

The far slope had come alive with dancing sparks as a hundred concealed rifles cut loose of full automatic. It looked like an exploding scoreboard after a home-team touchdown.

McKay was up again, leaving Gooding spitting out dust behind a bush, racing for the vehicle. Fire Team Charlie was reacting without the slightest sign of combat panic. Shiloh had kicked open the rear gate of the Carryall, rolling out with his M-249 with a box magazine plugged into it and a couple of belts of 5.56 wound around his shoulders. He was raking the hill with fire as he hit.

His buddies were coming out armed, slapping camouflaged Kevlar coal-scoop helmets on their heads. Matlock tossed McKay his big M-60 machinegun as he dove for the ground. DeWayne Burdick handed off O'Neal his M-16, mounted with a fat M-203 grenade launcher beneath its barrel. McKay turned and blasted a quick burst from the hip, hanging onto the pistol grips front and rear as though the hog were a giant Tommy gun, before joining the others in making serious love to the Northern Mexican *caliche*.

Mindful of how vital transport was out here in the middle of this hostile, barren landscape, Jimmy Jack Roebuck stayed with the vehicle, whose engine had chosen this moment to give up the ghost. The big Carryall groaned and rocked as he pumped the gas pedal frantically. The engine refused to catch.

McKay slapped down the bipod on the M-60E3 and tried to flatten himself behind it. He clamped the steel buttplate against his right shoulder with his left hand and sprayed the sparkling slope two hundred fifty meters away. Though the Maremont-made weapon was called "lightweight" in the brochures, it was only ten percent lighter than the full-dress M-60 and spat out full-powered 7.62 millimeter slugs with enough force to shoot through most buildings. It was a lot more intimidating than Shiloh's little 5.56-mm squad Automatic Weapon.

Somehow even its awesome roar and the cloud of dust and dried vegetable matter kicked up by its muzzle blast wasn't much comfort to Billy McKay, who was acutely aware of being caught in the kill-zone of as lovely a U-shaped ambush as he'd ever seen.

As if in reply a machinegun opened up from the ridgeline.

It was deeper-voiced than the distinctive popping of the ambushers' M-16s, and from the nasty high rate-of-fire snarl to its bursts McKay guessed it was a Belgian-made FN-MAG, in the same general weight class as his chopped 60. Whoever was jockeying the bastard didn't have a clue how to use it right; instead of squeezing out short bursts the way McKay and Shiloh were doing he was just holding back that fucking trigger, letting a whole belt go in a long yammering spray, risking a tangled belt or barrel meltdown.

Unfortunately, he had the smarts to walk the bullets onto the nearest big target. The sturdy metal skin of the Carryall rang as if a dozen dwarfs were suddenly pounding on it with ballpeen hammers, and the glass exploded from it in a crystal spray. McKay heard Roebuck scream.

Señor López's body was sprawled face down on the blacktop, quivering to the impacts of incoming rounds. McKay squinted through dust and the late-morning sun, searching for the telltale cloud of debris his opposite number had to be throwing up. He wasn't bothering to aim his own fire right now, just hosing the bad guys on general principles. In an ambush like this the first priority was to establish fire superiority over the bad guys, or at least denying them of it. Which meant you had to try to make them duck first, the ultimate game of chicken.

If only they had Mobile One, the V-450 Cadillac Gage Super Commando armored car that had served as their combination command center, mobile fortress, and home since the One-Day War. The firepower of the .50-caliber machinegun and the fully automatic Mk-19 grenade launcher mounted side by side in the one-man turret turned the waddling ten-tonne beast into a fire-breathing monster, ideal for ambush-busting. But no, they had to leave it behind. Too conspicuous, Washington said, as if three trucks loaded down with eighteen whole *gringos* weren't goddam *conspicuous*.

On his own Dr. Morgenstern had pointed out that the high-tech equipment and especially the computer codes in the on-board database were a bit valuable to risk a thousand klicks inside a foreign and quite possibly hostile country, which made sense, especially since the codes they'd captured when they grabbed the current Mobile One to replace their lost original

had enabled them to penetrate the communications of the entire
FSE. Anyway, if the thing busted an axle in the middle of
Mexico, hundreds of miles from any of the caches dotted around
the U.S. pre-war in preparation for their mission, they'd have
to junk it. So even McKay agreed it was best to leave it in San
Antone.

Still, he missed it pretty keenly right about now. He concentrated on trying to scope out that cocksucking MAG—

Steve O'Neal jumped up from cover by the roadside and
sprinted toward the Carryall. Fire Team Charlie was all firing
back now, and McKay could hear caps being busted behind,
where he guessed the other two teams had deployed. These
Texicans were shaping up Number One under fire. He'd have
to buy 'em all a beer—in hell or Mexico City, as the case
might be.

The incoming rifle fire stopped as if a switch was thrown.
The FN continued to roar, chewing at one of the deuce-and-a-
halfs now, but it was playing solo.

There was nothing mystical about the sudden cease-fire.
McKay had been expecting it. So was Steve O'Neal, who was
yanking at the driver's door of the Carryall. It was the natural
thing that happened when a bunch of yohos with crummy fire
discipline cut loose on full-automatic: all those thirty-round
mags ran dry in a hurry, and at just about the same time.

All this action had occupied less than ten seconds—it just
seemed like ten years. The loyal, trustworthy, helpful, and
obedient Colonel Gutiérrez was just grinding up the face of the
far hill.

A white sea-anemone of smoke exploded in the open cab of
the four-wheeler. McKay had the impression of wild flailing
motion at the core of the spiky cloud, and then the gas tank
blew in an orange and black rush. One of the Guardians left
behind—Sloan with his M-203 or Rogers with an M-79—had
popped a 40-millimeter white phosphorous grenade right on
top of the car. It nosed off the road and stopped. Flaming
figures staggered from it and collapsed, their shrieks clearly
audible. McKay hoped one of them was that fucking Gutiérrez.

The FN-MAG shut down. Whether the gunner was freaked
by the grenade or his piece had malfunctioned McKay couldn't

tell. Even Gooding was aware that the hostile barrage had stopped. He got to his feet and stood staring wildly around, right out in the open—just in time for the firing to break out anew as the ambushers finished switching magazines. Corporal Matlock came flying out of cover and took the diplomat down. McKay heard someone grunt as a round went home.

O'Neal had finally battled the Carryall door open and was manhandling a moaning, blood-covered Private Roebuck out when the shitstorm hit again. Bullets pinged off the frame as O'Neal slung his injured man over his shoulders in a fireman's carry and headed for the roadside. From the corner of his eye McKay saw him stagger as he took a hit, and another and another. He went to one knee, fought upright, lurched forward out of sight beyond the vehicle.

McKay realized he was into his third ammo box without having been aware of changing them. The plastic half-moons held only half a belt of ammo each, which would've been piss-poor in an ambush situation except they made it possible to fire just about full-out without an assistant gunner. The Belgian chopper hadn't kicked back in again. McKay decided not to worry about it any more and started looking for muzzle flashes to target on as more grenades began to unfold white smoke-blossoms on the hillside, courtesy of Sam and Tommy.

Casey Wilson tracked the heavy barrel of his rifle right along the ridgeline, hunting fresh meat. He was vaguely aware of admiration for the tenacity of the crew that had served that tripod-mounted machinegun. Though the ammo-carrier had seen the gunner and A-gunner both struck down, it had taken a bullet through the head to keep him from taking over behind the weapon.

Another cammie-clad figure appeared in the scope, crouched behind a bush and a black M-16. Casey barely bothered to pull in a breath and half-release it before squeezing; five hundred meters was an offhand shot for him. Nor did he bother to zero on his target's head or heart. A good body shot was all that was needed. In a way a gutshot was optimal: nothing like a buddy screaming in mortal agony to take the heart out of ambushers.

For a laid-back California kid, Casey could be a cold mother-fucker.

The target dropped. Relentlessly the long rifle moved on. Casey was breaking all the rules for good sniping. He was concentrating his entire being on his shooting, as a conscientious sniper did, but his two buddies were nowhere nearby. Instead they were spread out well to the sides and forward, trying to bring the distant ambushers within the four-hundred meter range of their launchers. His ass was hanging in the breeze; he could be had by a bad guy with a rock. He didn't even think of it.

Not even the flash and delayed boom of the second truck blowing up broke his concentration. He found another enemy, aimed, fired. The man doubled over. He caught a glimpse of a brown face contorted in agony as he swung away.

It was like his first kill, when his AIM-9L heatseeker flew right up the right tailpipe of a MiG-29. The Fulcrum had flown on for another ten seconds, apparently unharmed, then suddenly disappeared in a huge orange ball. The Syrian pilot never punched out.

Now as then he couldn't let himself think about it.

He only kept looking for more living flesh to receive the death he was meting out in 150-grain increments.

Special Duty Squad 551 had a pair of grenade launchers of their own in action, helping the two Guardians work over the facing hill with white phosphorous grenades and CS gas. It was a nasty mixture. Not only were the grenades pulling a smoke screen between ambushers and the killing ground, they were scaring the shit out of the bad guys. Nobody anywhere was happy at the prospect of being dusted by a WP round with flakes of burning metal that clung and ate their way into you like relentless alien bugs. And most of the Mexican soldiers had no way of knowing the choking, stinging CS wasn't some kind of horrible poison instead of plain old tear gas. Some of them threw down their weapons and booked.

But being in ambush gave you a sense of security, a sense of holding the upper hand. Even though they were getting slammed for a lot more casualties than they ever dreamed, the Mexican regulars knew they had their victims in the kill-zone.

They hung in and kept on busting caps.

Certified public hero though he was, McKay really hated what had to come next. There was ultimately only one way to bust an ambush—At least if you couldn't call on artillery more studly than four crummy forty mike-mikes.

Wishing they had Mobile One even harder than before, he jumped up, screamed, "Follow me! Let's go!" and went chugging up the hill, blazing away from the hip with his M-60 like Sly Stallone on speed.

Your usual technique for advancing under fire was fire team rushes, one covering while the others charged. Right now everybody was too pissed off for finesse.

They went rampaging up through a smoke screen already dissipating in the wind. The rapidly diffusing CS brought tears to their eyes. They just screamed louder and fired at anything that moved.

Sudden Sam was keeping pace with McKay as well as a younger man, though maybe the fact that the Guardian had to haul twenty pounds of M-60 gave him a break. The Ranger had a WWII vintage Thompson submachine gun, of all things. The Mexican who'd pulled the knife on Powell ran abreast of McKay with tears streaming down his leathery cheeks, firing somebody's M-16. One of his buddies came a few steps behind with an antiquated M-1 carbine. The survivors of 551 swept upslope behind them in a wide skirmish line while Sloan and Tom Rogers dropped 40-mm rounds just in front of them with surgical precision.

Hand grenades cracked. People screamed and jumped up out of bushes to flee. A soldier kneeling behind a yucca nailed the *norteño* carrying the M-1 with a burst. McKay stopped, braced, and just blasted the son of a bitch. The heavy bullets slammed into him, picked him up, and stood him upright before letting him collapse.

Then McKay was at the top of the hill. His lungs were burning out from exertion and forcing CS residue into them. He grounded the butt of the M-60 and went to one knee, panting and drawing in wheezing breaths of air that stank of blood and guts and burned gun oil mixed with the omnipresent dust. The ambushers were flying down the backslope while the Texicans threw shots after them, mainly to make sure they headed in the right direction. The fight was over.

Casualties were surprisingly light. Roebuck was dead, as was Matlock, who'd taken one in the head when he knocked Gooding down. Baird and Jaworcki from Alpha Team had been hit pretty badly. Two of the *norteño* guides were goners.

Steve O'Neal was still alive when they got to him. Just a quick check by Tom Rogers turned up ten separate entrance wounds. Had they wanted to prod him and roll him around a bit, undoubtedly they could have found at least a few more. But it was clear it was all going to be academic before too long. O'Neal would never live long enough to be dusted off, even if they still had nifty shit like rescue choppers and field hospitals. Tom slipped a sandbag under his head and tried to make him comfortable.

He managed a grin when McKay came dragging back. "You were right to be . . . paranoid," he whispered, though each word obviously sent daggers of pain stabbing through him. "It's up to you to carry on from here."

He twitched the fingers of his left hand, beckoning McKay close. "Give Marla my . . . love," he said. "Take care—of my boys." Then his head lolled to the side and he faded out from behind his sky-blue eyes.

"Shit," McKay said, for any number of reasons. Tom just reached down and quickly shut O'Neal's eyes with thumb and forefinger.

One truck had burned with a shitload of supplies, and the Carryall was a total write-off, of course. However, the retreating Mexican soldiers had thoughtfully left behind a deuce-and-a-half of their own. It was old, and hadn't been maintained too well, but it started right away when Casey tried it.

Though McKay was eager to get away from the killing ground as quickly as possible, in case reinforcements were on their way to aid the ambushers or the shooting had attracted the attention of a *Cristero* mob, the Guardians and 551 policed up as much of the soldiers' weapons and ammo as possible to replace what they'd lost and what they'd burned up. In spite of the loss of their leader the Texicans were hyper from their brush with death and their overwhelming victory; there were at least sixty enemy corpses strewn across the landscape. Sergeant Bill Warner had been all ready to start taking ears as trophies until McKay told him he'd kick his ass if he wasted time on crap like that.

There was one more thing to do. The Texican and *norteño* dead were wrapped in blankets and loaded onto the trucks with the survivors. It was maybe not the healthiest thing to do, but McKay came from an age-old marine tradition that you never left anyone behind. Not even your dead.

Then they fired up the trucks and drove on toward where their Mexican Tourist Bureau maps said a village should be located not far away.

CHAPTER
EIGHT ────────────

The village looked like something from a story by Stephen King.

Baird was in a bad way. He'd taken two rounds through the body. Hit in both legs, Jaworcki was doing better, but moving around a lot wouldn't do him any good. It wasn't likely that an out-of-way village in northern Mexico would have had the facilities to help a lot even before the *Cristeros* came to town, but perhaps the locals could at least supply a couple of beds to stick the injured in while the survivors figured out what the hell to do next.

The country was broken tableland; unless you were on the ridgetops you couldn't see far, and even from the heights there was a lot of dead ground. It was no sweat to park the vehicles in a gully about a klick from where the village should be.

"If the locals are hostile, they already know we're here," Sudden Sam commented, standing by the trucks glumly stroking his mustache. The short late-winter day still had a fair ways to run, but shadows had already pooled deep in the declivity. It was cold.

The diminutive *norteño* who'd been so quick with his wits

and his knife back at the ambush site shook his head. "They are not hostile, except to *Cristeros*. And if *los Cristeros,* they still are here, they know not the country well enough, you see?"

McKay grunted and sent Casey up to the top of a hill on one side of the little steep-walled valley and Shiloh with his M-249 and DeWayne Burdick playing A-gunner up the ridge on the other. Then he had Tom drive on afoot with Richard Gallegos from Toliver's Bravo Team and the small indige, whose name was Raúl, to scope the place out.

Tom was reluctant to leave the injured, but McKay and Sloan could keep an eye on them as well as he could, and in case of emergency use their sophisticated but extremely limited stock of medical gear about as well. In the meantime, someone had to make sure the place wasn't crawling with *Cristeros*—or soldiers from the late Colonel Gutiérrez's outfit, for that matter. And he was the best scout there was.

The three called back in forty-five minutes. "C'mon along, Billy," Tom said. "There's nobody left here."

Rogers's usual soft-voiced delivery kept McKay from feeling the full impact of what he said until the trucks rumbled into the village. What the former Green Beret had meant was that there was nobody left there *alive*.

Not wanting to ride under canvas in this alien, ugly land, McKay was holding down the shotgun seat in the lead vehicle with Casey Wilson at the wheel, too occupied with keeping the ancient U.S. Army surplus truck in motion to try hotrodding it. McKay had his M-60E3 between his knees, all ready for trouble. It wasn't that he distrusted Rogers; if Tommy said the ville was clean, then that was so. But trouble could always be arriving at the same moment they were.

But trouble had been and gone.

The first thing they saw was what appeared to be a scarecrow hung on the front door of a boxy little adobe hut. As they got closer a strangled sound emerged from the base of Casey's throat.

What they'd first thought was a scarecrow was the body of a little girl, pinned to the door by a pitchfork. She had dried there slowly in the Mexican winter sun. A skull face grinned horribly from between two black braids that flopped this way and that in the wind.

"Jesus," McKay said around his smoldering stub of cigar.

There were bodies everywhere. So many that the bounty had apparently overwhelmed the desert scavengers, the vultures and coyotes; most of them looked pretty intact. What appeared to be pitiful small bundles of rags and sticks lying in the streets or stacked against the mud brick walls suddenly revealed their true identity in a glimpse of mottled skull with scraps of hair clinging to it, or a wizened claw of a hand protruding in supplication for mercy that could only come long too late.

The advance party was waiting for them in the tiny dust patch of a *plaza,* the market square. Richard Gallegos sat on a rock with his head between his knees. Raúl's dark face was enigmatic as a Mayan idol's.

"Must have been a hundred, hundred fifty people in the village, Billy," Rogers said matter-of-factly. Bad as this was, he'd seen worse. So had all the Guardians. "We found eighty-odd bodies before we gave up counting. They made a clean sweep, near as we can reckon."

Special Duty Squad 551 was deassing the canvasbacks. The squaddies came out blustering and slapping each other on the back, still high from the busted ambush.

"Crap, what a crummy place," said big Tandy, swinging his fat-barreled M-79 back onto his shoulder. "What is all this shit lyin' around here?" He kicked a bundle of rags. A skull went bouncing away four meters and came to rest grinning right up at him.

"*Shit!*" he screamed, leaping back and swinging the grenade launcher down as if to blow the relic away. "Shit, look at that! Shit!"

"They're everywhere," Toliver rasped. He'd been riding shotgun in the other truck. Shiloh dropped to his knees and shot what remained of that dawn's breakfast of bacon, beans, and biscuits.

"C'mon, you pussies," Warner bellowed, jumping down from the back of a deuce-and-a-half. "Get your asses in gear and secure this dump."

Looking green around the gills, his squaddies complied. McKay wandered over to the village church. It was a blocky building with thick-looking walls. Sudden Sam rapped on one with a scarred knuckle. "Built these places solid," he remarked.

"Used to do double duty as houses of worship and fortresses against the Indians."

"Looks like they still do," Casey remarked, blinking through his yellow shooting glasses at fist-sized craters in the walls where divots of adobe and lumpy whitewash had been knocked out by gunfire.

Moving into the interior, McKay realized how solidly the place really was built: "Shit, these must be almost a meter thick. Hard core."

They hadn't done the job, though. Heavy beams had been lugged laboriously down from the mountains God knew how long ago to hold up the roof. A fierce fire had gutted the church and burned right through them, so that their blackened stubs lay angled down among charred pews.

"Shit," McKay said, running a hand along a fallen beam. "Didn't they leave anything?"

"Some places they busted up all the furniture, the plates and shit, everything," said Gallegos, who'd followed them in. "Like a buncha kids vandalizing an elementary school. Just for no reason at all. Other places they just left alone. I never seen nothing like it." He shook his head, made as if to spit, thought better of it. This was still hallowed ground, after all.

"They didn't leave any food," Rogers said. "Cleaned the ville out. Near as we can tell they killed out all the farm animals. Pigs, chickens, even the dogs."

"Like fucking locusts," McKay said.

Raúl showed a bitter smile. "We Mexicans are very, what you say? Frugal. We don't let things go to waste."

McKay scratched the back of his bull neck. He'd had a Texican barber trim him up high and tight just before they left. The stubble was itching back there.

"What's your last name, anyway?" he asked the *norteño*. "I feel funny just calling you 'Raúl.' Sounds like you're a bellhop or something."

Raúl shrugged. "What does it matter? I have no family anymore. Why do I need a family name?"

McKay frowned. "Where are you from?"

"Maybe here. Maybe that was my daughter you saw pinned to that door." He looked down at his sneakers. "Or maybe that girl was one of the lucky ones."

• • •

They found a few buildings set a ways apart from the others, relatively nontrashed. There were deaders in them, of course, but the cool, dry winter they'd been lying in for a month or six weeks had just sort of dried them out; they didn't stink all that much, and moving them out was about as little unpleasant as that kind of experience ever could be.

The 551 squaddies set out Claymores and trip flares and rigged cans on strings in hopes they'd warn them if bad guys began sneaking up on them after dark. The Guardians had carried some miniaturized motion sensors along—the kind of Star Wars toys McKay and Rogers, who'd seen how seldom the fancy high-tech stuff that got written up in *Popular Mechanics* actually held up in real-life combat situations, had distinctly mixed feelings about. They had to admit most of the tricky stuff Major Crenna had scared up for them performed to spec, or nearly so.

But that was all pretty academic, since the neato-keeno Robert McNamara people detectors had been in the truck that went to Jesus. And the wind kept rattling the goddamned cans, so they were going to have to rely mostly on their sharp-honed eyes and ears and hope no coyotes triggered any Claymores.

A Buck Rogers item that had survived was the portable satellite receiver/transceiver set, with the fold-up antenna that looked like an inside-out silver umbrella. McKay actually loved that one; it was similar to what his man Arnold and the boys had used in *Predator*. Of course, the piece of gear in that movie that really made McKay come was the amazing portable Gatling gun Jesse "the Body" Ventura got to carry around. Of course, if you actually tried to hand-fire a minigun you'd take off like a SAM-7 Strela after a jetliner, which was why he didn't have one instead of the Maremont.

Dr. Jacob Morgenstern, newly confirmed director of Project Blueprint, happened to be in when McKay called, shortly before sundown here in lovely Chihuahua.

"We been set up," McKay said without preamble, "big time."

The doctor listened in silence to what McKay had to tell him, but it was a very loud silence, the sort where you could feel anger sizzling right out of the headset. He told the Guardians to sit tight while he spoke to some people. When he rang off

McKay felt the strong temptation to go outside and watch for
the glowing trails of ICBMs arcing toward Washington.

After that it was time to chow down and let reaction set in.
Time to speculate about what had happened. And what would
happen next.

The Texicans got very surly. Bill Warner seemed to blame
the Guardians for what had gone down, though he never just
spat it on out. He and a Chicano jock named Lucero, who was
what remained of his fire team with Jaworcki and Baird all
racked up, sat to one side making these sideways comments at
each other. A couple of times, as darkness came down as if it
never planned to leave, McKay had the notion to invite one or
both of them outside to talk it over, but every time when he
was getting ready to engage his mouth and disengage his brain
Tom would catch his eye and shake his head.

The other squaddies were just pissed off at the world as a
whole. They had loved O'Neal, and as the hot-blooded
exhilaration rush of having blasted their way out of the kill-zone
subsided the pain came surging in to fill the gap.

"How could they do that to us?" Tandy kept asking, over
and over. "We come down here to help them. What they want
to fuck with us for?"

"They're sensitive about foreigners coming in here with guns.
Especially us foreigners," Sudden Sam said. He sat crosslegged
cleaning his Thompson and staring at the camp stove set in the
middle of the hard maroon floor.

"Well, then, what the hell are *you* doing here, then, Mr.
Ranger Man?" Lucero snapped. Heads came up; the Texicans
had not been overtly hostile to the Federal Texan before, just
wary, like strange dogs encountering each other on neutral turf.

"My job," Coates said quietly. "I was told to come down
here and help you people get along, since I got some experience
in this line of country."

"Hey, well, you did one hell of a good job, didn't you,
brother?" Lucero said with a flip of his head. He had these
very sculpted features and a short brush of hair. He came from
what was called a good family, which McKay gathered was
one with money, and he didn't make much secret of the fact
that he considered most people to be beneath him. "I wonder

if maybe you just didn't set that up, yourself, huh? Colonel Gutiérrez was a big friend of yours, you said."

"Hey, yeah, son, you done found me out. I got so much confidence in the marksmanship of the Mexican Army I reckoned they could dust your skinny asses without creasing a hair on my head."

Lucero stood up off the table he'd been perching on. "Listen, brother, maybe you and me—"

"Will you for fuck's sake shut up, Lucero?" said Buck Toliver, the Bravo Team leader. "I'm tired of that shit."

"Who the hell do you think you are to give orders to one of my men?" Bill Warner said, going red in the face.

"Why, hey, Bill, you wanna order me not to interfere when our people get to fighting among themselves, I guess you can just fuck me. And let the *Cristeros* slide in here and cut our throats while we're all going at it."

Warner scowled. He also backed down. Toliver wasn't as tall as he was but every bit as broad, and maybe then some. He was older than the other Texicans, McKay's age, early to middle thirties. He had a dusty, hardbitten way to him he'd picked up as a kid working the oilfields outside Odessa. He described himself as "part white trash, part Cherokee, part nigger, part Meskin, and all mean." He had a voice like five miles of dirt road, courtesy of too much whiskey and too many cigarettes and the odd forearm shiver to the throat during his college football career. From what the others said he'd made sergeant in the Marine Corps. More than once, McKay guessed—just like he had.

About then Baird came awake on his makeshift pallet by the wall and started moaning. Tom went to bend over him. The air was getting pretty thick in there. McKay slipped out and went to the next hut over where Sam and Casey were.

Sloan was sitting in the corner talking to the indiges, Raúl and this kid Miguel, who looked to be about fourteen. Miguel didn't have much to say; he kept looking off in other directions and blinking back tears with long feminine-looking eyelashes. It struck McKay he was about the only male Mexican he'd seen on this trip without a mustache.

Powell Gooding was there, too, his *GQ* grooming frayed.

He sat by himself staring at the insides of his eyeballs. He'd been pale and twitchy after the ambush. Tom had given him some Valium or some damn thing to keep him inside his skull. Apparently the diplomatic service wasn't working out the way he'd anticipated.

When McKay entered, Sloan came over to him. Casey, sitting next to the lantern in the lotus position, nodded absently to McKay and went back to meditating. But Sam was having an attack of the liberal guilts, and McKay had to at least pretend to listen.

Tom came in with Sam Coates just as Sloan was saying, " . . . feel terrible about what happened. Those two men died, and we barely even knew their names."

Tom looked at him with his head tipped slightly off-center. He shrugged. "They were indiges."

"How can you talk that way?" Sloan hissed, flipping his eyes back to see if the Mexicans were listening. Raúl sat smoking, and Miguel was weeping at the wall. "They were human beings, for God's sake."

"They were indiges," Tom repeated. He sounded genuinely puzzled.

Sam started to fill up with air for a big denunciation scene. "Hold on, son," Coates said. "Lieutenant Rogers was a Green Beret, wasn't he? A-team, cadreman. That kind of thing."

Sam frowned.

"That's right," Tom said.

"That's the kind of attitude you have to have for that line of work, Commander. It's like being an EMT, an ambulance boy. You just can't afford to care. You see?"

Sloan chewed the inside of his lower lip. That didn't satisfy him, but Coates had reminded him to be sensitive and caring about Tom as well as the semi-nameless corpses cooling under a tarp next to the huts. He could chase his own tail about it all night. It was kind of like Casey's meditation, the way McKay saw it. Gave him something to do with his mind besides worry about what a mess they were in *this* time.

"I'm going to go check the perimeter," Tom said. Casey came back from wherever he was, unfolded himself, picked up his sniper's rifle, and went out with him to help sentries Shiloh and Richard Gallegos stare holes in the night for a while.

That left the other three to stand around in silence for a spell while the wind whined around the *vigas*. McKay found himself staring down at the floor and sort of digging at it with the metal-reinforced toe of his combat boot. It was the same as in the other hut, hard and red and a bit shiny, like tile, but a continuous coating, too lumpy.

"What's this floor made out of anyway?" he asked.

"Blood and dirt," Sudden Sam answered casually.

Sloan stared at him in horror. McKay felt a sudden urge to levitate. "You mean these poor fuckers bled all over the ground and it turned into this?" he demanded. That was too gross even for him.

"No, no. The peasants take cow's blood or whatever and pour it on the ground, mix it up into paste with the dirt and smear it around, then let it harden. It's durable, and cheap, and folks moving around on it keep it shiny, give it a nice look. These are proud people."

But McKay and Sloan were making faces at each other like a pair of Valley girls confronted with a derelict who'd just filled his pants.

"I get the cot," McKay said firmly.

Morgenstern came back online a little after 2300. "If you can hold out there another thirty to forty-eight hours, I have help on the way."

McKay stared at the radio, seeing a whole new procession of unwanted bodies trooping in-country. As it was he'd been feeling a guilty satisfaction that the expedition had been trimmed down.

"We don't need company, Doctor," he said.

"No, I don't mean reinforcements, McKay. I'm well aware of the unwieldiness of your current party. I'm speaking of evacuating your casualties back north of the border."

"Well, hey, I'm all for that." He'd been wondering what the hell to do about Baird and Jaworcki. They obviously could not be moved far, and the group was sure as hell not going to infiltrate clear to Mexico City carrying them along. Out of their earshot Warner had been making noises about cutting their throats and driving on. That would be the big macho thing to do.

McKay could see his point, much as it griped his ass to flirt with agreeing with the former Ranger. Back with SOG-SWAC he'd made that same decision more than once, on missions deep inside enemy lines where there was no chance of extracting casualties who couldn't make it out under their own power.

But the time wasn't right. It wasn't as if they were hung out to dry in the *Dasht-i-Kavir*, ass-deep in Iran; they were just barely in *Mexico*, for Chrissake. The thought of adding to the friendly body count this early on a mission as fucked-up as this was turning out to be just stuck in McKay's throat.

"Well, okay, roger that, Doctor. But the world is still wondering why this great ally Washington set us up with decided to try and scrag our asses."

"Washington says they're as much in the dark as you. They've no idea as yet as to whether he did this on his own or someone got to him."

"Great. Terrific. Come to think of it, Doctor, these little gnomes you've got coming in to give us a hand—"

"Are my assets," Morgenstern said firmly. "My personal assets."

McKay looked around at his three fellow Guardians' faces hanging over the radio like pale balloons in the feeble green luminance of a glowstick. They were sharing the same thought, that Washington was compromised somehow. It was unthinkable, pure paranoia—except that it had happened before. But that had been cleared up, the leak exposed.

Still, Morgenstern's words were comforting. His personal network was impeccable, and extended into the damnedest places.

"All right, Doctor. We'll hold here two days. But no longer. This mission's supposed to be urgent. And somebody's liable to come looking for us if we hang out in one place too long."

"Move if you have to, but keep me apprised. Washington is giving top priority to investigating the ambush.

"I can't tell you how much better that makes me feel, Doc. Guardians out."

CHAPTER
NINE ─────────────────────

Baird died during the night.

The morning was windy and chilly, with clouds piled up white over the mountains. Since sunup everyone had been taking turns picking and scraping seven graves out of the cement-hard soil—with the exception of Powell Gooding, who'd come out of his funk enough to make it clear that grunt labor of that sort was beneath his dignity. They buried them in an onion field, which was allegedly easier to dig in than just any patch of desert because it had been cultivated. Digging those graves made McKay glad he wasn't a farmer, particularly one in northern goddam Mexico.

It got done, it all got done. By about ten o'clock they were ready to lower the seven dead men wrapped in makeshift shrouds of cloth scarfed from the village. Casey and Sam Sloan kept watch on a couple of hilltops overlooking the village and its dry, derelict fields, to free up the 551st boys to attend the burial of their comrades.

Tom read a few words from a tiny pocket Bible he always carried with him, while the wind whipped at the bloused legs of his camouflage coveralls. He was the religious member of the Guardians; Sam Sloan was very into being an intellectual, so naturally he was an agnostic, though he didn't push his views on Rogers, as just Rogers didn't try to impose his brand of Christianity on his buddies. Casey you just couldn't tell about—he probably worshipped Buddha or something, he was definitely into New Age stuff, reincarnation and healing energy and that kind of stuff, though McKay could never be sure how seriously he took it.

For his part, McKay was a lapsed Catholic who believed intermittently in God. Mostly when he was drunk; then he flashed back on how the nuns would tell him back in school that God was always watching when he did anything bad, which was frequently. He had been pretty devout, for example, the hungover morning after the going-away party in San Antonio. He'd alternated praying that his swollen head not fall off his shoulders and explode as he went through the motions of final preparation with praying for God to take him right on up to His bosom and put him out of his misery.

Now he stood with his head bowed and his Guardians cover—just a cammie boonie hat, not one of the nifty dark gray dress berets, which they hadn't brought along—held in front of his belt buckle as Tom read. He was very conscious of Raúl and Miguel standing off to one side. He felt bad they didn't have anyone to do a Catholic ceremony for the two Mexican dead. That wasn't like him; this fucking mission was getting to him.

He pitched in with a shovel when it came time to cover them up. He was ringmaster for this traveling circus, but somehow he didn't feel like pulling rank to get out of this task.

When the graves were filled in they wandered back into the village. Most of them sat around the trucks drinking water from the well, purified with some of Tom Rogers's wonder pills, of course, while a couple trudged up the hills to relieve Sam and Casey on watch.

"I wish I had a beer," Tandy remarked sorrowfully, sitting on the hood of the Texican truck. He held up his plastic one-liter water bottle and sloshed it around.

"Shoot. Wish I had me a six-pack," Shiloh said, lying on the hard earth with his head against a tire.

"Wish *I* had a case," Buck Toliver commented. He was checking over his Remington 3000 pump shotgun. It was his backup weapon; it had survived the blowup of the deuce-and-a-half because he'd grabbed it as well as his M-16 when Gutiérrez's boys popped their ambush and he bailed out. "Drink it all myself. Wouldn't even offer to share with you sad sacks."

"You always was a greedy motherfucker," Tandy said.

Gallegos had the hood of the Mexican vehicle popped and was rooting around inside. He was a pretty skilled mechanic. He was one of those people who always had to be doing something.

"What I wish I had," he remarked, "was a case of Tab."

The assembled troopies made gagging sounds and stuck their fingers down their throats. "You be keepin' that shit all to yourself," Tandy told him. "Offer it around, somebody be shootin' your ass."

"What I always hated," Shig said, "was this stuff called Diet Rite. My mom used to drink it." He shuddered. He was a square man with a round head and a flattop that tended to stick up in front, and hornrim glasses.

"What about caffeine-free Diet Pepsi?" Toliver rasped. "What the fuck was that supposed to be? Brown water?"

"This is brown water," Tandy said, squinting dubiously into his bottle.

McKay laughed. "Don't sweat it, blood. Stuff Tommy puts in there makes them microbes curl up dead."

Shig made a face. "All those chemicals make me nervous. I never ate anything with preservatives in it, before the war."

"You ever think they might be preserving you?" Tandy asked. "Hey, I like my germs dead. Hey, now. Thought of all those little amoebas squirming around in my stomach and dividing and shit makes me wanna puke."

"But it's not natural," Shig said.

"So what's natural? Dyin's natural; nothing be more natural than being dead. I want to live forever."

"Picked the wrong outfit to sign on with, boy," Toliver said, working the action of his pump gun.

"Watch who you call 'boy,' peckerwood. I call Washington, complain to the civil rights people."

"Fuck, Tandy, don't do that," McKay begged. "Maggie Connoly'd have a commission down here taking depositions from everybody before you knew what hit you."

"How about the way we busted that ambush yesterday?" Shiloh asked. "They cut loose on us, I thought we was goners. Hoo-*ee*."

"They picked the wrong people to mess with, my man," Tandy said. "We hard-core."

"Air*borne*," Shig declared.

"Chairborne," grunted Toliver.

So naturally that started the boys blowing and blustering about how *bad* they all were. Casey and Sam wandered down off their hills and came to listen in.

"How did we make it out of that, McKay?" Sloan asked. "There must've been a company of them up there. Why did they retreat? How *did* we win?"

"Huh?" McKay said intelligently. The heat of exertion had worn off in the cool restless wind, so that he had gotten to enjoying the feel of the sun on his nose and heating up the breast and thighs of his coveralls where they touched his skin, which was to say he was dozing off.

"Listen, to start with, we lost a third of our people in that fight. It's not like we won the battle of Antietam or anything."

"Sharpsburg," Shiloh corrected. McKay scowled at him.

"But we were badly outnumbered, McKay," Shig said defensively. "You have to admit that. And those were soldiers. Regulars."

Standing next to the truck Gallegos was dissecting, Sudden Sam laughed. He'd wandered over to join the party shortly after Sloan and Wilson arrived.

"They had uniforms, all right, so they must've been soldiers. Draftees, mostly, 'bout half-trained. Got some outfits that're pretty sharp in the Mexican army, veterans of kicking the ass of the Nicaraguans and Cubans that tried to invade out of Guatemala after the War," Coates said. "But not these boys. Spent all their time getting laid and running squatters off peoples' lands for hire."

McKay gave him a hard eye. Coates was a likable old coot for the most part, but when it all was said McKay didn't trust a Texas Ranger much more than the Texicans did. Not after the fun and games they'd had with Randy Jim.

"I thought these dudes were old pals of yours," he said.

Coates shrugged and commenced to roll himself a smoke.

"Well, shoot. Eloy and I worked together a few times. He seemed like an okay guy. But you know, we always did kinda reckon he ran protection for the *traficantes* a lot of the time. Called us and the DEA in to help out when the drug-runners wouldn't pony up." He stuck his cigarette in his mouth and lit it.

"Those things will kill you," Shig said earnestly.

"Well, hell, son," Coates said, shaking out the match, "life's fatal. Didn't yet know anybody got out of it alive. Did you?"

McKay took his turn on the hill with his M-60 and a pair of binoculars that afternoon. The landscape reminded him of this old horrible blanket he and his brothers used to rumple up to make a battlefield for their toy soldiers to reenact the battles they saw on Walter Cronkite, Khe Sanh and Hamburger Hill and all of them. It was a ratty old thing, filled with holes and long since faded from whatever color it had been to a stone-ugly grayish tan. The way this country folded this way and that all around was just like that old blanket-battleground, and it was pretty much the same color. It freaked him out that people lived here, or had before the *Cristeros* came through, anyway. The gritty grimy streets of Pittsburgh were bad enough, but jeez—

The sun was falling into the Sierras when Private Lucero came up and sneered at him and relieved him. He walked down the slope holding the 60 by the muzzle brake and carrying the piece back over his shoulder. It felt as if it was cutting his trapezius muscle in half. Of course, it never felt any better when you humped a pig like that, but the point was he was unaccustomed to it. They were getting soft, riding around in Mobile One all the time eating freeze-dried rations—well, most of the time. Maybe he ought to take the Guardians on a hundred mile hike or two when they got back, just to remind themselves they were soldiers and not commuters.

That's if we don't have to hump the rest of the goddam way to Mexico City, he reminded himself.

There was a figure standing on the outskirts of the unnaturally quiet village, waiting for him. He nodded as he approached.

"Afternoon, Mr. Gooding," he said, keeping his voice neutral.

Gooding had on a Pendleton shirt and jeans today. His hands

were in the pockets. His round cheeks seemed to have sunk in on themselves a bit.

"It's all your fault," he said, almost in a whisper.

McKay pulled up short. "What say?"

"You heard me. You killed those men."

McKay felt his cheeks start to glow. "What the fuck are you talking about?"

"You panicked back there. If you hadn't acted so precipitously they never would've opened fire."

"Are you nuts? They were laying for us. If Casey hadn't spotted them up on that ridge we would have driven right into the eye of the ambush. They'd have cut us down at point blank range. None of us would've made it out."

Gooding shook his head and laughed a bitter, strange laugh. "Squirm on the hook, McKay. Go ahead. Dr. Connoly warned me you wouldn't be as stupid as you appeared. She said that sometimes you're quite resourceful, and this bears her out."

"Thank her too fucking much."

"You blew it this time. I'm blowing the whistle. You lost your head, and our mission was fatally compromised before it even got properly under way. I shall make a full report when I get back to Washington. And believe you me, mister, it will be heeded."

"Well, you just do that, Captain Georgetown. Let them go ahead and fire my ass. I could use the rest. Maybe I'll sue for two years' back pay."

He hitched the MG higher up on his shoulder and stomped past the diplomat. He thought he heard Gooding laugh, but maybe it was just a trick of that coyote wind.

CHAPTER
TEN ————————————

At the last possible second, Cipriano Fuentes, chief of the Mexico City police, stifled a belch. Had it happened during a lull in the conversation, the sound would have chased itself up the heavy rafters of the great hall, echoing and re-echoing his shame. Fortunately, there were no lulls in this conversation.

The would-be powers that be were meeting up in Chapultepec Castle. They had none but the vaguest, incidental connections to the senators and deputies who had been earnestly arguing over what should be done in the wake of Córdoba's assassination ever since it happened down in the National Palace. The National Congress was a debating society, nothing more. Real policy would be made up here on the heights of the Hill of the Grasshopper, above the murkiest and smelliest of the pollution that socked in the enormous city.

It was an emergency session of the de facto government of Mexico. Servants clad in stark black and white uniforms glided beneath high chandeliers that blazed vigorously in defiance of the sundown curfew that blanketed the city, considerably less comprehensively than the smog. He hoped no one would take him to task over the frequent and flagrant violations of the blackout, which could not be suppressed even though power was shut off to the entire city promptly at sundown, at least in theory. Fortunately, the *jefes* and main men gathered here tonight had more pressing business on their minds.

"We can confirm, gentlemen," said General Barelas, rising from his ancient wooden chair with its high, ornately carved back upholstered in red velvet, "that an invasion force from the United States of America has entered our blessed motherland."

A groan rose from the assembly clustered around the long oaken table. Barelas held up a hard hand. "They were met in battle and severely battered by elements of the Third Division in Chihuahua, but managed to avoid destruction."

"A disgrace!" someone shouted. Barelas's face hardened.

"I assure you, the invaders will shortly be brought to battle and driven from our borders. It is only a matter of time."

Denunciations of the faithless *gringos* rattled around the hall like loose cannons. Taking advantage of the tumult, Fuentes thumbed a third of a roll of Rolaids into his hand and popped them into his mouth, camouflaging the motion as a concerned thumb-and-forefinger stroking of his mustache.

When his hand was safely back on the tabletop with a pen in it, he chewed the tablets and swallowed them. He hoped the Americans would be able to start manufacturing them again. The burdens of his office had long since ruined his digestion. The stores of the invaluable medicine recovered from the ruins and brought south by *norteamericano* traders would last only so much longer.

Cipriano Fuentes was a fat, greasy, thoroughly unattractive man. He recognized these things and felt no sorrow for them. He was also completely lacking in ambition. Paradoxically, that was why he was in such an exalted—and, on such turbulent evening as this, dangerously exposed—position.

During the precarious 1980s, when the world as a whole was flailing on the brink of the pit it fell into in the '90s, the chief of police for Mexico City was a man named Arturo Durazo Moreno. Durazo was a bad man. He wasn't simply corrupt, he was flagrantly, *flamboyantly* corrupt. It wasn't a matter of taking bribes and kickbacks and diverting public funds, though he was indiscreet enough about those activites to raise eyebrows in a country in which they were regarded as an implicit part of government. The problem was, he was an up-front gangster, who didn't hesitate to use the undercover goons of the Department for the Prevention of Delinquency as personal hit men. He was so bad that when he left office the book a former aide wrote about him rocketed to the top of Mexican best-seller lists and stayed there forever.

Eventually the situation got embarrassing enough for the PRI that they decided to install a hard-shelled pillar of virtue to run the cops in the Federal District. That was a disaster, too. Underpaid police officers couldn't augment their incomes with modest *mordida*—the bite. They took their frustrations out on the populace, aggravating popular resentment inflamed by the unprecedented interference of the new chief's hard-charging elite—well-paid, incorruptible, and overbearing—in all phases of everyday life. Without *la mordida* as a social lubricant to smooth interactions between people and police, nothing got done whatsoever.

So just when the biggest city in the world got terminally gridlocked, along came Córdoba's coalition party, who determined that what was needed was someone who would cause no problems one way or another, and most of all, not get greedy. And so, round little Fuentes, who from his humble beginning as a traffic cop determinedly yet self-effacingly clinging to his choice turf (a stop sign hidden by shrubbery) had always gotten along by doing his job methodically without pissing anyone off, found himself top cop.

It was the sort of compromise characteristic of Córdoba and his party: a middle path between morality and reality. By allowing his men to line their pockets as tradition permitted and survival demanded, but drawing a clear line at where *mordida* was acceptable and where it wasn't, Fuentes had cut down on serious crime and social upheaval alike.

Unfortunately, the coalition had died with Córdoba. Now while the big men struggled for position, the most the small could hope to hang on to was life itself.

Fuentes's stomach lurched again. Maybe his dinner was disagreeing with him. That was all he needed. If he had to give up hot *chorizo*, life would no longer be worth living.

•　　•　　•

Not bothering to pretend to listen to his colleagues' bloodthirsty declarations of what the *norteamericanos* could expect at their hands should they not cease their violation of sacred Mexico at once, General Barelas signed for an aide hovering discreetly in the doorway. He briefly whispered in the lieutenant's ear. The crisp young officer whipped smartly out.

Barelas felt sweat squeezing out along a hairline that was showing no sign of receding, and required only a modest investment in Grecian Formula to maintain in pure, virile blackness. *What on earth did that moron Guitérrez step in this time?*

Communications in post-holocaust Mexico weren't what they used to be, and that was never much. But rumor moved as swiftly as it ever had. From what Barelas's intelligence staff had been able to piece together, Gutiérrez had tried to dry-gulch an American regiment, which had pushed his face in. Some stories had it that the colonel had had the good taste to get himself killed, which would be the best thing for all concerned. Particularly *Coronel* Gutiérrez.

The whole thing stank to the Blessed Virgin. The *gringos* had problems of their own; the only reason they'd have for sending soldiers into Mexico was to do something about those fucking crazy *Cristeros*. If it were done quietly it was the best thing that could happen for Mexico, to exterminate those lunatics. *If*—trust the ham-handed Anglo-Saxons to send in a regiment, when any fool knew that nothing pissed off the *campesinos* quicker or more thoroughly than armed foreigners sticking their noses into Mexican business.

And what was Gutiérrez thinking when he jumped them, for Mary's sweet sake? He'd always sucked up to the *norteamericanos*. Barelas shook his head. There was dirty work being done here, and it wasn't all in Mexico.

The lieutenant rematerialized at his commander's elbow. He reverently set a glass on the table by Barelas's neatly pressed uniform sleeve. Barelas nodded briskly and the lieutenant vanished.

Barelas sipped, felt the reassuring burn of good Russian vodka. He didn't think his rivals needed to know just how much booze he was knocking back this evening. So he wasn't going to advertise the fact by asking the quiet, starchy servants for refills.

He believed in attending to details such as that. That's why he was suited to rule Mexico, instead of any of these *rateros*.

Eyes like a lizard's followed General Barelas's emptied glass in its arc toward the tabletop from behind planchets of mirrored glass. *Whom does he think he's fooling with his little games? Does he think I don't know it isn't water in those glasses his aide keeps bringing him?*

The huge, pitted face showed no emotion. Known as *la Araña*, the Spider, to his enemies—he had no friends—Apolinar Morales never showed emotion, except when it suited him to. Most observers tacitly assumed that whatever emotions filled that dwarf's outsized head set upon the body of a stone-muscled man of normal height were unpleasant. Mostly they were correct.

"I can only applaud the patriotic sentiments that have been aired here," the general was saying, "and echo them. I assure you the Americans will be punished for their effrontery."

A gray tongue moistened lips as bold and hard-edged as a blaze cut from a pine tree by two strokes of an axe. Morales tipped his dished face forward. "Laudable," he said in his rasping, sinister whisper. "Quite laudable, General."

He settled back and sipped from his own glass. It really was water. Whatever his vices were, he didn't see fit to share them with his present associates. Heads had turned toward him with the sort of horrified, exultant expectation shared by spectators at the *corrida* during the millisecond of realization that the bull wasn't fooled by the cape.

Like any good *matador*—or any good bull—he hated to disappoint his public.

"But the Ministry of the Interior intends to more than applaud and echo, my friends. Or even assure." When he said "Ministry of the Interior," it was of course understood that he meant the dreaded Federal Security Directorate. Morales was officially here as the subordinate and representative of the minister, himself on permanent vacation in Acapulco behind high walls and Belgian-made rifles. The wise pretended to believe it.

"We intend to act."

"Brave words," the general said sourly.

"Brave *deeds*," Morales murmured. "The situation demands

no less, don't you agree? Though I understand how you, as a military man, feel the need to wargame all the possible contingencies before taking action. That's commendable caution, of course."

The others didn't quite gasp, but he felt their appreciation of the neat way he'd emasculated Barelas. He accepted the unvoiced sentiment graciously, as befit an artist.

"At this moment, we have special details from both the Directorate and the Federal Judicial Police"—which he had snapped up last week, during the disorders caused by the approach of the *Cristero* horde—"closing in on the invaders. Dodge as they will, they won't elude my men."

The listeners did gasp, this time, at the audacity of it. It was a lie, of course; his people had no more idea where the invading *gringo* battalion was than Barelas's drones. But it was a lie in good faith. He had no doubt his men would turn up the intruders long before the army got its thumb out of its butt. He'd read the dossier on Eloy Gutiérrez, and had an idea of the caliber of men Barelas had to work with.

"But more than that, we are prepared to act decisively to remove the menace of the *Cristeros* from the outskirts of our city. This threat has been countenanced for far too long. Security considerations forbid me to discuss specifics, of course, but I may say, our measures will be most vigorous."

That woke up that flatulent little toad Fuentes. The awareness he was about to be attacked in his sanctum penetrated his fat skull. Morales didn't care; there was nothing he could do about it, save maybe dig his own grave deeper.

"How great is the threat, really, Colonel Morales?" the police chief had the temerity to ask, emitting little belches about every third syllable.

"How can you ask that?" the representative of the Secretariat of Commerce and Industrial Development asked in shrill outrage. Commerce was the last bastion of the conservative PAN, long since discredited by rumors of American government involvement—rumors substantiated in part by evidence Morales himself had either turned up or made up, as circumstances warranted. "The heretical rabble are thronging to the city! There must be tens of thousands of them!"

"Hundreds of thousands," agreed the Health and Public Assistance man—rare enough, since his secretariat was a PRI holdout. "Do you forget, Chief Fuentes, that we had that odious Señor Tejada before us only yesterday, threatening us with the stake—yes, with medieval torments—should we not make some unwashed slut from the provinces empress of Mexico. Perhaps an emergency disbursement of welfare—"

"Begging the gentlemen's pardons," Fuentes said, spooling a handkerchief out of his pocket and mopping at his forehead, "but there's a million squatters between the *Cristeros* and us, even after the bomb and all the sickness. They threw back the fanatics once already, when they tried to force their way in yesterday. Why might they not do so again?"

"If Chief Fuentes is doing his patriotic duty by admitting his inability to control the rabble," Morales said softly, "we could certainly find the charity to accept his resignation in order that a more dynamic hand should take the reins."

"And one of your toadies would supply that hand, no doubt," Barelas sneered. "Small chance."

Fuentes wadded the handkerchief and jammed it into the breast pocket of his uniform, where it ruined what line his tunic had. "I just think the situation may resolve itself. This is Mexico, not the North, where people are always driven to be *doing*. Here we know that time smooths everything down. That's all I'm saying."

"Indeed," Morales said, permitting his lips to curl into the sneer that seemed to be their natural state. "Your reminding us of what it means to be Mexican is appreciated, *Jefe*. But I can't help but ask, what if the great leaders of our past, Father Hidalgo or Emiliano Zapata—what if *they* had been content to wait for time to solve the problems that confronted our nation?"

The great face swung away. "Gentlemen, have we any further business?"

The meeting began to break up. The participants studiously avoid Fuentes.

Damn that ogre, that horrible pockmarked creature, he thought, and pressed fingers to his moist purplish lips to contain a burp. Morales meant to hound him to his doom, he knew. It wouldn't be enough for him to resign—as if he'd ever wanted to be chief of police anyway! No. Morales intended to drink his blood.

He shivered. Maybe literally. The stories they told of the secret police boss back in the days when he was with the White Brigade, the super-secret government unit which fought leftist terror with terror during the late Seventies, was enough to turn a stomach less delicate than his own.

The country was falling apart. Rotting away from the inside and collapsing in on itself. Enrique Córdoba had seen that and done what he had to. That was to surround himself with a cult of *personalismo,* something Mexican politics had been painstakingly constructed to avoid after the chaos of the Revolution. But with the fall of PRI and its strongest rivals, the old system had failed. Córdoba had shored up the nation with his own overwhelming personality.

And now he was gone. The roof was caving in quicker now—maybe quicker than if he'd never existed. Fuentes had worshipped Córdoba. But now he was unsure whether to bless his memory or damn him to hell.

But one way or another, he wasn't going to roll over and present his pouchy throat for that misshapen monster Morales. To a creature who perversely gloried in having a feminine noun—Araña—for a nickname, which any real man would find an intolerable affront to his *machismo*. If the path of cowardice was closed to him, then he would have to choose courage.

The great hall was empty now. He squared his shoulders and put a hand on the flap of his holster, which held a gun he'd never fired. *What's Chona put out for my snack?* he wondered, and waddled toward the door with as much dignity as he had within him.

CHAPTER
ELEVEN

Jacob Morgenstern's promised aid hadn't materialized by dark, so the Guardians laagered in for the night. The Texicans put two men on lookout on top of the taller of the hills overlooking the village, a thirty or forty meter height so symmetrical Sam wondered whether it was a volcanic cinder cone. They were there under orders from 551's new boss, Corporal Bill Warner.

The call had caused some dispute. Because there were so few of them, both Tom Rogers and McKay wanted everyone to stick together inside their little two-hut perimeter. An observation post up on the hill couldn't possibly be supported in case of attack. And there was enough natural cover and dead ground surrounding the village that if the hypothetical bad guys had clue one as to how to use cover the hilltop's height advantage wouldn't help a bit.

Warner's service time had been spent in the jungles of Central America. He laughed out loud at the idea that there was sufficient cover in this barren landscape for people to sneak up on the village without being spotted by his keen-eyed troopies.

McKay tried to order him not to set out the OP. It wasn't

the right move. Warner got on his back legs and snorted a lot about how he was in charge of the 551st Special Duty Squad and just because they were allies didn't give the Guardians the right to throw their weight around and just who the hell did McKay think he was, anyway?

McKay wanted to take the bull-necked ex-Ranger outside and show him just who the hell he was. But naturally the squaddies pulled together behind their buddy and now leader, and Powell Gooding started carrying on about how McKay was imposing on a valuable ally—as if his pal Maggie Connoly wouldn't soil her bloomers at the idea of recognizing a secessionist government. The clincher was Tom catching his eye and giving his don't-push-it headshake. The fact was they had no authority over the Texicans and needed their cooperation if this fucked-up mission was going to go anywhere other than hell. So Billy McKay got to eat the shit of giving an order he couldn't back up.

He did the only thing he could: made his own arrangements and went to sleep.

"Oh, my God, they're everywhere!"

A scream in his headset and a hysterically protracted burst of automatic weapons fire from the hilltop raised Billy McKay right off the cot he'd claimed.

In about half a second McKay was in a sitting position with his Maremont in his hands, trying to kick the thin blanket off his legs. "Tom, Sam, Casey—report!" he said, subvocalizing so as not to give his position away by shouting.

"I've got intruders on the sensors," Sam returned from the other hut. He had a little battery-powered backup monitor for their fancy motion detectors.

As he was speaking McKay heard the characteristic *thump* of a 40-mm grenade launcher fired nearby. A second or two later harsh blue light came pouring in the windows of his hut.

"Who did that?" McKay demanded.

The roar of a nearby explosion swamped the reply, even though it was transmitted directly through his skull by the bone-conduction phone taped behind his ear. "Say again!" he said, hauling the M-60 up and shoving it through the window next to the low doorway.

"I did, Billy," Tom replied. "I'm on the roof." He meant the hut next door, which he shared with Sloan, Gooding, Warner, Shiloh, and the injured Jaworcki.

"We have company."

The machinegun on the hill had stopped. Gunfire was popping off in the middle distance. In the garish light of the parachute flare Rogers had popped McKay saw dark figures converging on the two isolated huts like wolves.

He sensed motion in the room behind him as Casey and Toliver's squaddies came awake and started feeling their way to their battle stations. This was your large economy-sized *campesino* hut, with not one but two rooms. The Texicans were pretty quiet, he had to give them that, and moved surely, with no sign of fumbling around.

A tidal wave of light crashed across McKay's field of vision to the accompaniment of shattering noise.

The flitting figures came apart before McKay's very eyes as hundreds of steel marbles tore through them. Rogers had triggered the Claymores set in a swastika pattern around the huts with an electronic hand detonator, a clacker.

For one breathless moment there was silence. Then McKay imagined he heard—or maybe he felt it through the khaki-colored mud brick of the wall—bits of debris thudding back to earth, guns and severed limbs and other assorted body parts. Screams of wounded intruders began to filter through the ringing the Claymores had left in his ears.

A shriek in his headset almost tore his head off.

"Who was that?" he demanded. Out in the artificial light, which was already strobing erratically as the flare began to gutter out, he saw bodies littering the hard-packed earth. Some moved. Most didn't.

"OP, Billy," Tom replied.

"Shit. What was that explosion?"

"Dynamite bomb. Some guy got overeager with the fuse."

Sudden Sam was at his side, tommy gun in hand and toup awry. *"Cristeros?"* the Ranger whispered.

"How'd you guess?"

A quick grin. "Their trademark. That bomb. Dates back to the original revolt in the Twenties. Your Meskins are mighty traditional-minded people."

• • •

Sam Sloan came up with his Galil-203 at the window, intensely aware of what Billy McKay called the Pucker Factor: it felt as if his entire ass was about to collapse into his sphincter. He peered cautiously over the splintery wood sill at a scene out of Dante, broken bodies lying where the Claymores had left them in the unreal light of the dying flare. Behind him he heard Warner yelling into his radio, trying to raise Burdick and Lucero in the OP.

Sam heard a rasp of leather on blood-stabilized mud, and then he felt himself torn away from the window. Powell Gooding had his hands wrapped in the slack of Sam's coveralls.

"What are you doing, you madmen?" he gobbled in Sloan's face. "Can't you see those are our allies, the help Morgenstern promised us?"

Sam was mostly concerned to hang on to his weapon. The 203 was off safety, and if it dropped and went off the Multiple Projectile round would fill the one-room hut with a lethal spray of buckshot.

"What?" he said intelligently. He really wasn't tracking what the State Department man was saying to him. He was too focused on expecting a soft-lead slug from some ancient *Cristero* Winchester to catch him just above the bridge of his nose.

Gooding's eyes stared from his face. The juice drained out of his Wolff System tan, and dark stubble stood out stark against his ashy skin. He shook his head, quickly, spastically, like a terrier breaking the neck of a rat, and spun away. Sam snapped back to the window as if attached to a spring, expecting to see the dusty street brimming with *Cristeros*. Fortunately none was in sight but the dead or soon to be.

Gooding grabbed Warner by one thick arm. "You've got to do something. They're killing our allies!"

Warner slammed down the microphone; the radio was bringing in nothing but static from the hilltop position. He brushed the diplomat savagely off. " 'Allies,' my dick," he snarled, and from the 7.62 crack in his voice Sloan thought he might hit him. "Those're dinks, and they're about to start coming in over the wire."

He grabbed up his own M-203 and went to cover at the other window.

For ten minutes nothing happened. A wounded *Cristero* had dragged himself—or herself, who knew; they came in both flavors—into another hut and lay crying, a shrill, edgy sound that sounded like a horny cat. The screaming went down the backs of the defenders like ice water, until a couple of Toliver's troopies started discussing trying to pop a grenade onto the wounded *Cristero* to shut him up.

"Negative to that," their corporal rasped. "They gotta like it a lot less than us."

The next voice McKay heard was Warner's. The Guardians' second channel was tuned to the 551st Squad radio so they could keep touch with their comrades. The words rang in his head and crackled from Toliver's walkie-talkie, sitting on the one heavy table, half a beat out of snyc.

"I want to take a team out to the OP," the Texican said.

"Negative to that." Feedback squealed in McKay's head. He grimaced and dialed down the gain on his throat mike with his left hand. His right never strayed from the pistol grip and trigger of his M-60. "Christ knows how many of those bastards're out there. They'd nail you before you went thirty meters."

He could feel Warner getting hot from twenty meters away. "Dammit, those're my men—"

"They wouldn't be out there if I had my way, Warner. Fucking forget it. What the hell are you asking me for? I thought you didn't have to take orders from no blue-belly like me."

He waited for an angry outburst from Warner, or quiet reproof from Tommy on the scrambled Guardians channel, letting him know he'd overplayed his hand. All that came back was a subliminal carrier-wave buzz.

Raúl huddled at the rear of the room by the firing slit they'd knocked in the back wall that afternoon to give them 360 degree coverage, with his M-16 in his hands and his silent kid companion beside him. That had been a much harder task than McKay would've guessed—these adobe things may have looked like Cubist turds, but they were built to goddamn *last*.

"They have a trick if they catch you, *los Cristeros*," the *norteño* said. "If they feel, you know, playful, they stake you above the spike of the *maguey* plant."

Glancing over his shoulder, all McKay could see was a gleam

of the kid Miguel's frightened wide eyeballs in the starlight scattering in the window. The moon had gone down hours ago. Of course.

"Yeah? That don't sound so bad."

Toliver gave off a rock-tumbler chuckle. He squatted next to a window in the other room. He had an M-203 in his hands and his pump gun leaning conveniently against the wall right next to him. "*Maguey* spike's a real hard and horny stalk. Grows a couple of feet in a night, right time of year."

"Shit," McKay said, with feeling.

" 'Course, this is the wrong time of year for that. They catch you, they'll probably just pull all the skin off you and hang it off a *maguey* to dry, like they do their laundry."

"Christ on a crutch, Toliver, are you always this goddamned cheerful?"

"Usually he worse," Tandy said.

"Something's moving," Richard Gallegos hissed. At the same instant Rogers called a warning from the roof next door.

McKay heard the thump of Casey's suppressed rifle—you didn't "silence" a full-powered 7.62 load, just quieted it down some. "Saw a face in the hut opposite," he explained, adding apologetically, "I think I missed, man."

McKay just had time to remember Casey's quirk of being virtually unable to hit targets inside fifty meters, and then muzzle flashes boomed out right in his face, some so close he felt the hot push of them, and the night filled up with figures screaming, "*¡Viva La Vigren! ¡Viva Cristo Rey!*"

His own muzzle flash flared out before him, big as a Subaru. The Maremont was nothing in comparison to the big .50 mounted in Mobile One, which he was missing again about now. But it was enough to send bodies sprawling with chunks of meat visibly flying off them.

In the split-second intervals between the Maremont's laddered bursts—three rounds, four, five, three again, keeping them short so as to lower the risk of a misfeed—McKay heard the *tick-tick-tick* of Shiloh's M-249 next door. Tom, Sam, and the two Texican noncoms swept the street with MP rounds that turned their grenade launchers into giant shotguns.

They had good if short fields of fire, and plenty of firepower. The rush withered like dry grass in a blow torch flame.

But the bad guys had infiltrated the nearby buildings. McKay ducked as a bullet gouged the windowframe, sending splinters into his cheek like fire-ant stings. Sudden Sam crouched beside him. He grinned wolfishly past the receiver of his old M-1A1, teeth white beneath his mustache.

A bullet cracked right through the glassless window overhead. "Sam, pop some Willy Peter on those dickheads across the street, will you?"

"Roger wilco, McKay."

" 'Roger wilco?' You actually said 'roger wilco?'" He shook his head. "You been watching too many war movies. Nobody says roger wilco. Jesus Christ, it's almost the twenty-first century. Get with the program."

For reply McKay heard the *whomp*! of the 203's hi-low pressure propellant charge. And a thud.

"Thud?" Sudden Sam hung his prominent nose over the sill like Kilroy. "Seems like there oughta be more to it than that."

"A dud," Sam reported bitterly.

"Negative, Sam." Tom said. "Range is too short. Won't arm." A 40-mm grenade had to spin through ten meters or so of free flight before it armed itself. Inside that distance it was just a big, blunt bullet.

"Shit. Start working over the buildings where you can do some good. I'll see what I can do." He took a cold stub of cigar from his breast pocket, stuck it defiantly between his teeth, popped up and fired a long burst into the face of the hut across the narrow roadway.

A satisfactory cloud of adobe dust billowed out, and he heard a scream and caught a glimpse of somebody's head flying apart like a watermelon dropped on the sidewalk in the nearst window. Just as soon as he came off the 60's trigger all these guns appeared in the windows and blazed back. The *Cristeros* were firing Vietnam style, holding the pieces up over their heads and shooting blind.

"Fuck," he said, ducking again. The jacketed 7.62 slugs wouldn't penetrate the thick walls of mud reinforced with straw. "Anybody good with hand grenades?"

"I am," Shigeo said.

"He's real good," Tandy offered. "Used to pitch for the Dodgers' farm club in San Antone. Got him a fine arm."

A Nip pitcher? McKay shook his head. In Japan, yes, but America? *Oh, well, that's what makes this country great.* "Great. See if you can strike a few of these pukes out."

McKay, Coates, and Gallegos all popped up on signal in the window and cut loose at the other hut. When the *Cristeros* had pulled their heads—or hands—down, they ducked and Shigeo threw a big M-34 white phosphorus grenade. The target was close enough that he just pitched the damn thing overhand, a neat curve that sailed cleanly through the blank black window of the building opposite.

There was a blue-white flash and smoke boiled out of the windows. There were screams and the sound of frantic activity. A burning man burst out through the front door. Coates dropped him with a three round burst. He lay there smoldering while the defenders' nostrils clogged with the stink of burning human fat.

Little white lights glowed in the interior of the far hut where the phosphorus flakes had been scattered around the walls. It looked like a planetarium to McKay, when the smoke started to disperse. Nonetheless, he had to duck back quickly as a couple of lucky and incredibly hard-core *Cristeros* who'd somehow escaped being dusted with the lethal flakes cut loose at him. Shiegeo had to toss in a pair of CS grenades before the building was cleared—for the moment.

Two hours later the *Cristeros* came on as if they'd never stop.

CHAPTER
TWELVE ─────────

For the hundredth time Sam Sloan caught himself just as his chin was starting to dip toward his chest. *Got to stay alert,* he chided himself. *I'm a Guardian, after all. Besides, I'd sort of like to live to see the sun come up.*

The earth shook, throwing him to the dried-blood floor. He never heard a thing. He was only aware of a rush of light and then lying there feeling as if his ears had been stuffed with cotton batting.

This is the way the world ends, he thought vaguely.

The explosion of the dynamite bomb right beside the hut had sent Tom Rogers sprawling. He grabbed at his Galil Short Assault Rifle, which had gone skittering across the roof like a frightened animal, and came up onto one knee, firing position. It was a dangerous way to expose himself, but this wasn't a moment for caution.

A scrawny figure appeared from beside a hut, arm cocked to throw a bundle from which hung a spitting fuse. Rogers fired a short burst. The figure sobbed audibly, dropped to his knees.

A heartbeat later he vanished in a shattering explosion.

McKay ducked as a dynamite bundle dropped in the street outside. The hut shook to the explosion, but the walls held. He forced himself to snap back into position, muscles of his face contracting in expectation of being blown off his skull. Instead he found himself firing into a fresh wave of attackers, so close the muzzle flames set cheap flannel shirts afire.

In the other room Toliver had used up his MP grenades and fallen back on his shotgun. He was firing into the crowd that suddenly pressed up against the walls when a hard brown hand shot up from below the window and grabbed the barrel.

Toliver hauled up and in with all his might, dragging a startled *Cristero* half his size right over the sill. While the Mexican blinked up at him, belatedly aware he'd made a bad mistake, Richard Gallegos shot him once through the body with his M-16.

Toliver put up a booted foot and kicked the limp form back out to his friends and relations. He grinned at Gallegos, who shook his head.

A figure loomed at the window, brandishing a revolver, Toliver fired from the hip. The upper right quadrant of the *Cristero's* rib cage opened up as if set on hinges, and he fell back out of sight.

Shouts and shots, sounding as if they came from a kilometer away, tugged at Sam's awareness. But his body did not want to respond.

Shiloh and Warner were firing from the other two windows. Gooding huddled near the wall. Sam thought he was saying to himself, "I'm a man of peace. What is happening to me?" over and over. But it may have been his imagination.

A sandal cut from an old tire came through the window and stepped on Sam's face. That did it. He grabbed the ankle, pulled the big shiny Colt Python from its shoulder holster and fired straight up into the open mouth turned down on him in horrified surprise. The *Cristero's* eyes bulged, and the top of his head unfolded like a flower in stop-motion animation. Blood and clots of brains showered Sloan.

Gagging, he twisted away from the corpse that flopped atop

him. Another blast went off not far away, followed by a wild shriek. Shiloh wheeled back from his window with a hand clamped on his face. Blood spurted between clawed fingers.

"—claymores, Sam," a soft but insistent voice said in his head. He realized it was Tom Rogers, realized his fellow Guardian was repeating himself. "Sam, are you okay."

"Oh, sure, I'm fine," he said in a voice that cracked like that of an adolescent propositioned by the head cheerleader. "Couldn't be better."

"The claymores," Tom said.

"Oh. Right." His hand groped out and found the clacker attached by wires to the mine they'd dropped out the window during the last lull. An arm reached in the window for him.

He pressed the clacker. There was a lot of light and noise. The arm dropped right into the room, drooling blood onto the floor beside him.

He stared down at the severed limb. *That should freshen up the finish on that floor,* he thought idiotically, then stooped to pick up his Galil.

The second set of claymores blew the attackers away from the two huts like a housewife blowing spilled salt off a Formica counter. As his ears recovered McKay was aware of a roaring sound somewhere nearby. He smelled burning canvas.

"Billy," Tom radioed, "the truck's on fire. The one between the huts."

"Shit," McKay said. They'd parked the two vehicles so they'd be as clear as possible of their fields of fire, one between their huts, one behind the larger one. It'd be a bitch to lose half their transport, but they'd get by. At least they'd unloaded their supplies.

"Billy," Casey said. He sounded worried.

McKay's teeth skinned back from his lips as he yanked open the feed tray of his M-60 and slapped in a fresh belt of ammo. For most people to sound worried under the circumstances was pretty normal, but Casey in his own flaky way was as imperturbable as Tom.

"Here they fucking come again!" somebody yelled.

"Jesus," Toliver said. "Can't they just leave pamphlets, like the Jehovah's fucking Witnesses?"

Raúl laughed. His face was blackened and one cheek had been laid open by a bullet. "They don't got to leave pamphlets. The *Cristeros* think everyone not with them, she damned already."

"Heretics," young Miguel spat. It was the first word anybody on the expeditionary force could remember hearing him say.

McKay came up to find someone standing just past his front sight. He pulled the trigger. The M-60 fired once, the bullet punching through the *Cristero's* sternum and sucking most of his lung-meat along with it on the way out. The machinegun jammed.

"Oh, fuck *me,*" McKay said plaintively. They were thronging around the door and window like reporters in the front yard of someone whose family just died in a plane crash. McKay dropped the Maremont and turned away.

"Billy," Casey said again, firing a burst from the Ingram submachine gun he used for close-range action.

A claymore lay on the floor nearby, with a fuse stuck in it with wires trailing from it and a clacker nearby. McKay grabbed it up, handed it through the window to a *Cristero* who was trying to clamber in the window. Startled, the man took it.

McKay put a hand on his chest, pushed. The man staggered two steps back into the street. McKay dived to the floor, jammed the wires against the clacker's contacts, prayed they were the right ones, and squeezed.

The explosion was pure music.

"Billy," Casey repeated insistently, "the *gas tank.*"

Oh, shit, McKay thought, *what the hell was I thinking about?* He was so happy they'd brought their ammo inside that he'd forgotten about the special ultra-high capacity tanks the Texicans had fixed their transport up with for the jaunt into Mexico. They'd topped off at a Guardians cache in southern New Mexico. The idea of fifty or so gallons of gas going off right next to him did not fill him with joy.

McKay's claymore seemed to have discouraged the attackers; those who could were falling back from the defenders' huts. *Cristeros* in the surrounding hut kept up a brisk fire that played on the thick walls like heavy-metal drummers.

Casey sprang from his window. Before McKay could say a word, he was past the ruined shreds of door hanging on their hinges and into the street, blazing bravely if wildly away with his MAC-10. Bullets kicked up little swirls of dust around his ankles and clouds of pink stucco chips from the hut's facade.

Shigeo appeared in the doorway, hurling a perfect strike in the door of the nearest hut. McKay stood up in the window, bellowing wordlessly and firing his machinegun from the hip.

The white phosphorus grenade exploded. Firing stopped from across the street. McKay hosed his bullets into another, much larger structure seventy meters away, the village cantina from which the bulk of the fire seemed to be coming. He heard the truck's starter groan briefly.

"C'mon, baby," Richard Gallegos breathed fervently, slapping a fresh magazine into his M-16.

The truck's engine caught, roared angrily. It shot out into the street, trailing a cloud of orange flame. The canopy was burning merrily, and the upholstery in the cab seemed to be on fire, too. McKay caught a glimpse of Casey hunched down behind the wheel, a black silhouette against Hell's open door, and then the truck was jouncing down the rutted street. McKay heard a steel-drum cacophony as bullets hammered it.

He threw a leg over the sill and came through standing and shooting past the truck. Raúl charged out the door firing from the hip. Toliver and company followed on his heels.

At the end of the street Casey bailed out, rolling from view with his coveralls burning merrily. The truck plowed into the cantina and exploded. Flaming gasoline flooded out like lava, swamping the cantina. Screams soared wildly above the pandemonium of gunfire and explosions.

Richard Gallegos hit the window of the nearest hut with a stun grenade. When it flash-banged off, Sam Coates rolled through the door as slickly as an instructor in an antiterrorist class. He killed a pair of *Cristeros* coming in from the other side with two precise bursts from his Thompson. Then he and McKay and Fire Team Bravo rolled up the block, slaughtering stunned *Cristeros* and driving the survivors before them like animals while their buddies laid down supporting fire from the smaller hut.

It was nearing dawn when they finished mopping up. Either there hadn't been all that many *Cristeros* to begin with, or these weren't as hard-core as some the defenders had encountered during the invasion of Texas.

"All that many" and "hard-core" were relative terms, however. The haggard defenders totaled over two hundred dead before even Bill Warner's body count fever played itself out. Of course, a lot of the casualties were still alive when they were found, too badly hurt to escape on their own. The *Cristeros* seemed to figure if you couldn't walk out it was up to God or the Virgin or somebody to help you; they'd gotten known in Texas for leaving their wounded lying.

The *Cristero* wounded were dealt with by a quick knife stroke across the throat. It was brutal but necessary. The expeditionary force didn't have the means to deal with prisoners, and they certainly didn't have the capability of treating enemy wounded, even if they'd had a strong desire to. They didn't have the facilities to take care of their own—and only the fact that Jaworcki's wounds weren't immediately life-threatening made him worth saving. Everybody in the party knew what it was like to be forced to put a buddy out of his misery—or hers, sometimes. Not even Sam Sloan protested at the killings. He forced himself to do his part, though his skin took on a grayish green cast and kind of sagged around his jawline.

It was pretty gross, on the whole. You could walk twenty meters in the open in any direction from the two huts without touching bare earth. The street had turned to a stinking, sticky mud blood.

"When this stuff dries, maybe it'll get a nice finish like them floors they got in the huts," McKay observed, lighting a hard-earned cigar as the sun peeked up past the broken land to the east. "Way I see it, what we done here is brought this town some urban renewal."

Sam Sloan made a gagging sound.

The total cost to the defenders had been one dead, one missing, and one seriously injured, leaving out innumerable bruises, cuts, contusions, and the singeing Casey had gotten before he rolled out the flames on his coveralls. It was scarcely short of a miracle, considering the hell they'd been through.

"A shining example of peace through superior firepower," Warner had called it. McKay had to agree with him again. Twice in twenty-four hours was almost too much.

The worst-hurt of the defenders, Shiloh was almost certain to lose his left eye, which Tom had treated as best he could. It hadn't stopped him manning his M-249 machinegun to cover the final counterattack with blood and aqueous humor streaming down his narrow cheek.

He was philosophical now, sitting on an orange crate with one side of his face bandaged over, smoking a cigarette and cleaning his weapon. He was waiting for his buddies to get back. As soon as the village was cleared Warner had taken the rest of his boys out to look for the two troopies who'd manned the OP.

A few minutes later they came dragging back in, looking grim, carrying the M-249 machinegun the lookouts had taken with them.

"We found Lucero, all right," Warner said. His face was suffused with angry blood. "He was naked. They'd cut on him a bunch."

"Looked like he was dead when they did it, anyway," Tandy offered helpfully. "Not much blood, and all." Warner shot him a poisoned glare.

"What about Private Burdick?" Sam asked.

"Gone."

Casey emerged from the hut, looking as if his high school science project had run amok on him. His face was smeared with white zinc-oxide ointment. One eyebrow was gone and the other looked none too robust. His longish blond hair had been turned to a mass of tufts of assorted lengths. Swatches of tender pink scalp showed through here and there.

"You're gonna have to shave that off," McKay said, studying him critically in the grayish early light. "We ain't gonna have no Guardians wandering around looking like they got the mange."

"Oh, no, Billy," Casey pleaded. "Like, don't make me do that."

"Being high and tight never killed nobody yet," Mckay said smugly.

"He gone have to be bald, get all that the same length," Tandy said.

"Maybe this'll help." Richard Gallegos came out of the two-room hut and handed something to Casey. The former fighter jock turned it over in his hands, almost reverently. It was his Dead tour cap.

"Thanks, man, thanks." For a moment Gallegos looked as if he was afraid Casey would try to kiss him.

"We need to get some rats inside us," Warner said. "Then we wanna head out again to see if we can find DeWayne. Any of you know anything about tracking?"

"I know some," Rogers said. He was up on the roof with his Galil, an M-79, and a pair of binocs.

"Maybe you don't want to find him, if they caught him alive," Sudden Sam said quietly.

"Don't give me that shit, you blue-belly loving Federal son of a bitch!" Warner screamed. "He's my man! I came in with him, I'm going out with him. Are you afraid, you cocksucker?"

Coates frowned. "A smart man learns to disregard those things a comrade in arms says in the heat of anger."

"Comrade in arms? You ain't shit to me. you don't like what I say, make me stop. Or don't you think you can take me?"

"Son, I believe man's a tool-using animal. I don't fight with my fists." Without being obvious he had squared himself, his right hand free in the general vicinity of the Smith & Wesson .41 magnum slung at his hip. McKay wondered suddenly just why they called him "Sudden" Sam.

"You don't have to bother going after Burdick," Rogers called softly from the hut's roof. He pointed off toward the hill where the OP had been.

Burdick stood there in the midst of a knot of small, armed men. There was something about the way they were dressed that struck McKay funny.

"Holy shit," Shiloh yelped. "DeWayne's done got himself captured by Apaches!"

CHAPTER
THIRTEEN ─────────────

"Burdick," Bill Warner called. "Are you all right?" The soldier said nothing, just stood looking down at his boots. His hands appeared to be tied behind his back.

McKay squinted. A band of clouds resting on the horizon held the light down, filtered it out. He wasn't sure quite what it was he was seeing.

"Yeah, wow," Casey said, trying to shift his tour cap around on his head so it would hide all the bare patches at once. "They look just like those old photographs of Geronimo and those dudes."

McKay knew as little as was possible to know about Geronimo and those dudes, and was perfectly happy that way. Now he noticed that Burdick's captors had long hair tied around the temple with headbands, and yellow stripes painted across their cheeks beneath their eyes. Maybe he had seen some pictures like that, come to think of it.

He felt the others shifting their weight uneasily around him. Apaches didn't have the best kind of reputation, at least not in all those cowboy movies everybody grew up on. But this was

the twentieth century, damned near the twenty-first . . . he
started noticing things, like that these men were wearing stuff
like Lee jeans jackets, and the stubby little rifles they held
were Soviet SKSs—or maybe ChiCom Type 68s, which were
real similar.

"What're we gonna do?" Shiloh asked, low.

"Get ready to scatter," Warner murmured. "We stay bunched
up, they can take us all out—"

"Stay cool," Rogers said, quietly urgent.

"But Apaches," Tandy said, "they real bad news."

"Now, I don't know much history," McKay said, "but I
know goddam well Geronimo didn't carry no Eastern Bloc
weapons."

A figure appeared over the hill, walking past Burdick and
his captors, down toward them with hands in blue jean pockets.
It had a black hat with an eagle feather in the band pulled down
over unbound hair that hung past the shoulders. The newcomer
was even smaller than the men holding the sheepish-looking
trooper.

McKay started walking to meet the figure, out of the little
village with its pervasive smell of death. He heard Warner sort
of growling behind him, apparently his equivalent of dithering.
If the former Ranger decided to follow him he hoped he
wouldn't bring any heavy hardware along to make his dick feel
big. McKay had long since figured out that whoever these people
really were, if they meant any harm they never would have
shown themselves.

He didn't know which way the former Airborne Ranger was
going to turn, but a current Ranger of a different kind appeared
by his side, loping along with an easy stride that belied his
lack of height, trailing blue smoke from a Bull Durham
cigarette. Sudden Sam grinned up at him. *Crusty old mother's
enjoying this.*

The newcomer stopped about twenty-five meters from them
and jerked a thumb backward over a denim-jacketed shoulder.
"That belong to you?"

McKay had gotten a good enough look at the figure not to
be surprised when the voice came high and feminine. What
did surprise him, a bit, was that it spoke clear English with

only a slight accent, more a difference in cadence than pronunciation.

"Yeah. Who the hell are you?"

Beside him he heard Coates cackle. "Hearts and minds," the Texan said, *sotto voce*.

The woman smiled thinly. She had a sharp oval face with high cheekbones and a flat nose. Her figure was spare but appropriately contoured.

"You come right to the point. No white-eyes bullshitting around. I like that. But maybe you should tell me who you are first."

"You ask the questions here, huh? All right. I'm Billy McKay, leader of the Guardians."

She looked him over with eyes as sharp and black—and hard—as obsidian arrowheads. "So you are. Right answer. I'm Judy Betzinez. I've come to help haul your pale asses out of the hot water you've stumbled into."

McKay jutted his chin and rubbed it with his hand. Stubble rasped—he had to remember to shave ASAP. "My turn to play twenty questions. Who sent you here?"

"A certain doctor, currently practicing in California. Used to perform surgery on ragheads in places like Mitla Pass and the Golan Heights."

" 'Ragheads?' You prejudiced against Ay-rabs?"

She stuck her hands back in her pockets and looked back up at him. *Way* up. She was tiny, maybe four and a half feet tall. "They got kicked off their land, just like us *ndéé*. They're still stuck in tent camps." She waved around at the arid landscape, starting to come alive in yellow and gold as the sun emerged from behind the hills. "We're back. If they can't do better than us savages, fuck 'em."

McKay jerked his head up the hill. "What about him?"

"He's okay. Just shook up some." She turned and called something in a language that was half chanting and half strangulation. One of the small men whipped out a small knife and slashed.

"Hey!" Warner shouted from twenty meters behind McKay. Burdick raised his freed hands as the severed rope fell to the ground, examining them as if they'd just turned up on the ends of his arms and he wasn't sure what they were. His captors took their Type 68s out of his rib cage and prodded him forward.

His teammates rushed stumbling forward to surround him. "DeWayne, my man, are you all right?" Tandy asked, grabbing him by the arm.

"I'm okay. Hey. I'm just shook up."

Shig blinked at him through his glasses. "Did they, you know—*do* anything to you?"

"Naw. Just found me wandering around. Tied me up 'cause they didn't know what else to do with me."

"Going to invite us in for breakfast, McKay?" Judy Betzinez asked. "If we're not wanted, we can head back to the Mescalero and let you wait here for half the Mexican soldiers, *federales,* and *Cristeros* in the world to hunt you down."

"Since you put it that way, why don't you stop in for a bite to eat, if you ain't in a hurry."

She nodded and started walking forward. As she passed him Tandy said, " 'Pale asses,' huh," under his breath.

She turned and looked him in the eye. "Listen, blood, you're all whitemen to me." She walked on and left him standing.

The squaddies crowded around Burdick like dogs around a man with a box of milkbones: "DeWayne, my man. What happened?"

He shook his head. His skin had wood-ash undertones. "I'm not sure. All I know is, all of a sudden there were like hundreds of these guys all around, just popping up right out of the ground, all around us. Eddie had the MG. We were shooting as fast as we could and he was hollering on the radio, and then there was this huge flash of light right in my face. It sort of stunned me, you know? Then when I could move again I couldn't see Eddie. I picked up my rifle and started firing, burned up a couple magazines, and then they were all over me. I started hitting 'em with my piece, holding on by the suppressor like my man Davy Crockett."

"What happened then?" Gallego asked.

DeWayne frowned at the ground. "I-I'm not sure. I just sort of went out."

Toliver touched the back of the trooper's skull. His fingertips came away tacky with mostly dried blood. "Somebody skulled you with a rock, bro."

Burdick shrugged. "Maybe. . . . Anyway, I woke up I was all alone, didn't have no weapon. All I had was this headache. I called for Eddie, but he wasn't nowhere. There was all this shooting. I—"

"Go ahead, son," Tom urged gently.

"I freaked, man. I—I just took off running. Then these little Indian dudes found me, took me captive."

Bill Warner had been standing to the side while his man told his story. Suddenly he lunged at Burdick, face almost black with blood. "*Coward!* You fucking *coward!* You ran off and left Eduardo to die!"

McKay stuck out his right arm and just clotheslined Warner. The corporal fell flailing on his ass in the dust. He bounced right back up, full of fight, but his men held him back from McKay and Burdick.

"Chickenshit! *Coward!*" He tried to spit at Burdick. He was totally off the wall, screaming like a school kid in a tantrum. "You ran away!"

Burdick had his hands up as if to fend off his leader's words. "He didn't have any choice," Sam Sloan said, outraged. "He was alone and unarmed. And there were hundreds of *Cristeros* all around, in case you didn't notice."

McKay nodded slowly. He had his eye on Warner beneath lowered brows, like one dog about to go for another who'd transgressed his territory. Actually, had it been him out there on that hill, he would've figured he had the fuckers outflanked. But he was a Guardian. You didn't expect some poor grunt to act like a Guardian. Didn't happen.

Warner raged a moment longer against the restraint of his men, then allowed himself to be led down into the village. The Apaches stood on the outskirts, watching with unconcealed amusement.

Corporal Buck Toliver hung back, sucking on a cigarette. "Funny thing about when we found Eduardo," he said to the air. "He had a buncha wounds inflicted after death. But only one that had bled much."

He threw down the cigarette and crushed it under his heel. "One bullet wound. In the back." He hitched up his M-203 and walked down to the village in his rolling gait.

·   ·   ·

The Apaches—they really were Apaches, too, from the Mescalero Reservation in New Mexico, though they insisted on being called Chiricahua, for reasons McKay had no clue of and didn't care to learn—were twitched out by all the dead *Cristeros*. As the day began to warm up, the air in the village got more than slightly oppressive, so they wound up leaving Tandy and Shig on watch in the ville, and moving back up the hill to heat their Lurp ration packs over brush campfires.

"So what's this about half of Mexico bein' on our case?" McKay asked with his mouth full. What he really wanted to ask was how the hell they ever got hooked in with Dr. Jake Morgenstern. On the other hand, he wasn't all the way sure he wanted to know.

"We've been listening in on shortwave to Mexican military and federal police traffic. They got the idea that a whole division of Americans has invaded. They are pretty comprehensively pissed off about it."

"But why?" Casey asked, sitting with his skinny ass on a thrust of feldspar. "We came down to help them."

The Apaches grinned at each other over that one. They all seemed to speak English pretty well, though they were quick enough to start slinging their own language when they didn't want the white-eyes to catch their drift. All things considered, McKay thought they were pretty much the same as anybody else, though awful small. Still, that paint made them look kind of creepy.

"They think you invaded, bro," one of them said. He was wearing a black Harley Davidson shirt beneath his jacket, which made the paint seem even stranger.

"Jesus," McKay said.

"We got a pickup truck to take your wounded back into the States to get treatment. But as for the rest of you—" She studied them critically across a mug of coffee. "We got to get you civilian clothes. And that's going to be a real bitch."

"Civilian clothes?" Warner said. "What the hell for?"

"Listen," she said, "under most circumstances a Mexican will only cooperate with authority under extreme duress. They're not like your suburban white collar types, can't wait to run off and do their middle-class duty to society anytime they see somebody cross against the light. *Nakai-yé*—Mexican—equate *authority* with *enemy*. They're smarter than you white-eyes, if not by much.''

Everybody looked at Raúl and Miguel, who were sitting with their mess kits, not saying much. Raúl smiled halfheartedly and shrugged. Miguel just stared into the pale flames and looked depressed.

''But they got a thing about foreigners. Especially heavily armed ones. They see you running around in your Rambo suits, dripping with weapons, they're going to freak right out. That's going to be enough to get somebody to turn you over, especially since both the government and the *Cristeros* want your butts.''

''If there's any difference,'' McKay said.

''Still is—for now. Your little incursion has stirred the pot down in Mexico City, and it won't take much of that to force the provisional government to hand the country to *Hermana Luz* on one of old Porfi Diaz's best plates.'' She knocked back a mouthful of scalding liquid. ''So you lose the cammies, unless you're looking to fight all the way to the Federal District.''

''So what?'' Warner burst out. He tossed a hand back at the ville. ''Look at the mess we made of the *Cristeros*. These little people can't stop us.''

''The *Cristeros* are fanatics,'' Tom Rogers said.

''So? That makes 'em harder core. As easily as we grease them, what we got to worry about a bunch of peasants for?''

''Bein' fanatical made the *Cristeros* nice and obliging about standin' in front of our guns,'' Sudden Sam said, poking the fire with a gray piece of driftwood. ''The *campesinos* are liable to be just as mean, only smarter.''

''*Cristeros* whipped their asses.''

''Lot more of them than there are of us, Bill,'' Toliver observed. Of all the 551 squaddies, he was the most likely to stand up to their new leader. The others seemed determined to pull together behind him no matter how big a horse's ass he made of himself. Laudable but misplaced loyalty, McKay thought.

''Meskins can fight mighty smart,'' Sam Coates observed. ''Whipped the French pretty well, back in the 1860s.''

Warner sneered. "What's the big deal, beating the goddam French?"

"That's what the 1st Cav brass always told us in the Nam."

"But surely we can explain our errand to the people," Powell Gooding said. He was still subdued, perhaps aware he hadn't made too good an impression during the battle for the village. "We can talk to them—"

"You talk to them, government man," Judy Betzinez said. "And while you're trying to make them understand your university Spanish, some kid'll be slipping out the back way to go for the *montañeros*."

"Who're they?" Sloan asked.

"Indians," an Apache said. "Not like us. *Mean* Indians. Most of 'em come from these little tribes way back in the hills, nobody ever heard of but some anthropologist. Federal police recruit them specially. They carry FN rifles and ride horses and hate everybody who doesn't speak their dialect. Shoot, half of 'em don't even speak Spanish."

"What a country," McKay said.

Judy Betzinez stood up and signaled to the people McKay had long since surmised were continuing to keep an eye on them from cover. "We'll get your injured man on the way home. And we'd better move out pretty briskly. *Cristeros* found you. No telling who else might happen along."

"Like all the *Cristeros'* friends and relations," Richard Gallegos said.

They were getting to their feet. "How much of our little Alamo did you see?" McKay asked.

"Just the tag end."

"Thanks for the help," McKay said.

"Hey," said one of the other Apaches, "no percentage in messing with those dudes unless we have to. Not for a bunch of lousy white-eyes."

"So you feel the mission has been compromised?" Jacob Morgenstern asked.

"I don't know," McKay replied, by way of the neat silvery inside-out umbrella, being aimed at a satellite by Sam and another of his magic black boxes. "We were definitely set up by Gutiérrez. But that coulda been because he figured this

Sister Light was gonna come out on top and he wanted to make nice with her. And there's a lot of *Cristeros* still wandering around this sandlot out here. This bunch *could* have stumbled across us by accident."

"But you don't think so."

"I don't know," he said again. "All I know is, my nasty, suspicious nature's got pretty worked up over what's gone down."

They had split from the village as quickly as they could. Most of the Apaches had taken Jaworcki and headed back north, leaving one party out trying to scrounge civvies for the expeditionary force and Judy Betzinez to help guide the Guardians and company to the capital.

If they decided to proceed.

That was the question the head of Project Blueprint was asking now. "If you decide to abort the mission." Morgenstern said, "I'll back you all the way."

"What about Sister Light?"

A pause. "We can hope that situation will resolve itself to our satisfaction."

McKay felt his lips spread out wide across his face in an expression nobody who wasn't legally blind could mistake for a smile. He looked at his buddies, who were perched among the rocks on the side of a high hill overlooking a broad valley. They looked back at him. It was his call to make.

"Negative to that, Doc," he said. "I just don't see us kicking back and sitting on our thumbs hoping everything'll work out. I think we all know how well that sorta thing works out. We're gonna go in and resolve the situation ourselves. But there is one thing."

"What's that, McKay?"

McKay moistened his lips and stared for a moment at the cloud-shadows chasing themselves across the landscape. This country seemed too big, somehow. It was too damned much for a city boy unused to being able to see more than a couple blocks in any direction.

"Washington is cut out. Completely. We don't deal with them, we don't answer to them."

"I'm not sure that's possible, McKay. You're aware I had to bend to pressure already concerning this mission."

"Well, Doctor, what I'm saying is, that has to end. Or the mission does."

Another pause. Just when McKay began to wonder if Sloan had lost the satellite link, Morgenstern said, "I still have to answer to the president."

Hell, you can give sitreps to Jeff. But don't tell him too much, you know? You're an old hand, Doc. I'm sure you can work out ways to keep him happy without spilling too many details."

Yes. I am at that. Very well; from now on, you report only to me.''

''And may God be with you.''

CHAPTER
FOURTEEN ─────────────

The squatters' camp was smoking devastation. The crazy-quilt shacks of cardboard and crates and flattened beer cans had mostly been trampled and burned. Bodies were sprawled everywhere among the smoldering heaps that had been crudely improvised dwellings.

Across the field a limousine waited, but *Hermana Luz* had insisted on walking the symbolic distance to the city limits herself. Now she trod on ashes that burned the soles of her feet through her tire rubber sandals, and her heart was sick.

Oh, Mother Mary, I had no idea.

Manuel Tejada trotted next to her, his alligator shoes sinking to the silken ankles of his socks in the ashy dust at every step. He was puffing, though they had walked but a hundred meters since dismounting from their own vehicle, a former schoolbus.

"Why, Manuel?" she asked quietly.

He frowned at her, his smudge-rimmed eyes screwed up with consternation. "Why what?"

She gestured around her with a small, strong hand. The gesture lit on the corpse of a middle-aged man twenty meters away, who lay on his back with his T-shirt pulled up under his armpits and legs outsplayed. A cane knife had laid open his big belly. Purple-gray guts looped out. A dog was tugging at them.

"This. All this killing."

"But they were heretics, *Hermana*. Godless swine who would not acknowledge your holiness. We destroyed them, in your name."

She shook her head. A group of her faithful stood with rifles slung, pointing and laughing at the dog and its grisly treat. *Who are these people who follow me? What are they?*

She preached peace. The infinite peace and love of the Brown Virgin, who spoke through her. Could the Virgin of Guadalupe possibly want her children to slaughter each other?

It had been so exciting, the throngs who acclaimed her, who chanted her name with the love beating up off their faces like heat-shimmer from a desert road. And that they would go forth, with her name inscribed on banners bearing the likeness of the Virgin of Guadalupe, to spread her message to all the world . . . it was a greater thrill than anything she had imagined in her short life.

But the world was a larger place than it had seemed to the shy, simple country girl from San Luis Potosí. And a much harsher one.

Three of them awaited her beside the huge, shiny limousines: a tall man in military uniform, a little fat man in a sweat-stained *policía* uniform beside him, and a very strange man with a long face dished and pitted like a crescent moon and sunglasses like mirrors. Reflexively she feared him.

Then she remembered who she was, and raised her head on her slender neck. She had been chosen by the Virgin, touched by Her hand. She had nothing to fear from the likes of this creature, demonic though he looked.

Also, several thousand of her faithful were marching a respectful distance behind her. She could see the men dividing their attention between her and the armed multitude that followed her.

As she approached the fat man removed his hat and knelt at her feet. "*Hermana Luz,* I am Cipriano Fuentes, Chief of Police for Mexico City. In the name of our city and the Virgin, I welcome you." He grasped her hand in moist fingers and kissed it.

"It is I who speak for the Virgin," she said, her voice high and clear. "But I thank you, Señor Fuentes. You earn much grace."

She looked haughtily at the other two. They cast glances sidelong at each other from behind their sunglasses, each waiting for the other to make the first move.

Behind *Hermana Luz* her followers made a noise. A low, collective growl, deep in many throats. The general and the man in the suit removed their hats and went to their knees as one.

She held out her hand for them to kiss in turn. But all she could see was that poor dead man, split open like a discarded doll before the ashes of the shack which had been his home.

"A Hawaiian shirt," McKay said in horrified disbelief. "*Bermuda shorts?*"

"Well, they don't have a lot of call in these parts for clothes for people your size. Or Corporal Warner or Corporal Toliver, either. What they have in your sizes is mostly for tourists." Judy Betzinez held up a shirt that looked as if somebody had drunk a lot of orange, black, cobalt blue, cerise, and yellow paint, and barfed it up all over it. She looked at it, then McKay. "I think it's you."

"Do you really think nobody's going to suspect us if we wear those?" Sam Sloan asked. "I mean, all these obviously fit young North Americans running in a pack—"

She shrugged. "I didn't say it was a good idea. *I* didn't dream up invading Mexico with a handful of white-eyes. Sure people are going to suspect you, but you go in wearing cammies, they're gonna *know*. You choose."

Toliver held an even more noxious Hawaiian shirt up in front of his broad chest. "Hell, I think it looks sharp."

"You set us up, Betzinez," McKay said.

She grinned.

The truck that'd blown during the fight at the nameless village had been the other one they'd brought in from the Republic of Texas. That was good because it started right off when Casey jumped into it at the battle's climax, thanks to the close attention Richard Gallegos had paid to it. But it also meant what they were left with was the one they'd picked up as booty from the Mexican Army. There was only so much even Richard could do with that one.

Still, it held up pretty well—at first. Even in the devastation the *Cristeros* had left finding fuel for it was not too much trouble. The fanatics frequently preferred to walk where they went. So, while they liked to burn Pemex stations, the only kind there were, as symbols of the hated Mexican government which ran them, some underground storage tanks survived with gas inside. Vandalism is a less compulsive motivation than greed or need; they got sloppy.

And there was fuel, even almost two years after the war. This wasn't *The Road Warrior*. Mexican oilfields hadn't exactly been a priority target during the One-Day War. Many were still hanging in there producing, and the refineries were refining away. In fact, the oil business was slumping, with the deaths of a couple hundred million of Mexico's best customers worldwide. The expedition managed to keep the tank topped off.

But as they passed south through Chihuahua into mountainous Durango the troubles began. They were following secondary roads that were supposedly paved, but the pavement was liable to go to Jesus at any time. With all the washouts the roads looked worse than most of the U.S. even after two years of complete neglect. In response to the rougher going the transmission began to grind like a rock crusher, the radiator started leaking, and the engine caught a shake that rocked the cab. As each new glitch got serious they'd have to ditch to the side of the road while Casey and Richard Gallegos fiddled with the beast, and the others stood around in their ludicrous tourist disguises, trying to pull security without being obvious about it.

McKay sat on a whitewashed rock overlooking a panoramic view of some wide valley. The sun was high and hot on his face, though the dry breeze blowing along the mountainside was cool. He was frowning at a small, rickety X of warped old slats perched on the rim of the drop-off twenty or so meters along the highway, trying to figure out what the hell it was for, when he heard a crunch of leather on gravel, and his hand moved reflexively to the stubby little H&K submachine gun stashed behind the rock.

But it was just Betzinez with some cold beans wrapped in a flour tortilla and a knowing smirk on her thin lips. Sheepishly McKay took his hand away from the hard-rubber grips of the MP-5. The weapons came in .45 caliber with silencers built in, specialized antiterrorist tools that had fortunately survived the catastrophes so far. They might come in very handy in Mexico City—*if* the expedition ever got that far.

"Nervous?" she asked as she sat on the rock next to his.

"Hell, no. Just tryin' to figure out what the hell that thing there is supposed to be." He jerked his head toward the wood X.

"That? A roadside shrine. Pretty chintzy one. Want some?" She aimed the business end of her burrito at him.

"No thanks. What do you mean, a roadside shrine? You mean like to Saint Christopher or something?"

"I thought the Pope said he wasn't a saint anymore. No. To somebody who went over the edge"—she gestured with the burrito—"about there."

McKay craned his neck. They were about two hundred meters up, and the slope was steep, studded with deceptively porous-looking lava rocks. "Somebody who went over—?"

She shrugged, tearing a bite off the end of her snack. "Car or truck, maybe even a bus. People drive like crazy things down here. Always going off cliffs."

"Shit. I'm glad we ain't seen much traffic."

"We will. We're coming out of the area the *Cristeros* hit worst."

"Terrific." They sat for a moment, listening to their own thoughts, and the muffled clanking and thumping and occasional "Shit" or "Oh, bummer" from Casey and Richard, and somebody whistling "Louie, Louie" with even less tune than the song usually had, all to the restless accompaniment of the wind.

"Your name's Betzinez," McKay said eventually. "You happen to know a guy named Jason Betzinez? Be an older guy. He was an Apache."

"Still is. He's my uncle."

McKay looked at her with one eyebrow raised. She grinned at him. "And you were the secret project he was working on."

"What?" If McKay had taken her up on her offer of a bite of burrito he'd have sprayed it all over the mountainside. Sergeant Jason Betzinez had been their physical-training instructor during Guardians training. He'd also been an old war buddy of the mysterious Major Crenna, who'd conceived the Blueprint and the Guardians. It was hard to imagine the stone-faced Apache breaking security, even with close family members.

"He told you that?" he demanded.

"Nope. Just worked it out for myself. All he ever told us was he was involved in some super-secret government program. He brought his old friend Crenna, the one-eyed dude, around to visit me once when I was at the University of Arizona a couple of years before the war." She shrugged. "Not long after that they had that article in *Parade* on you Guardian types. Mentioned you'd been 'trained extensively in the arid Arizona desert,' as if there's any other kind of desert in Arizona. I knew something about the kind of stuff Major Crenna was always getting involved in, and figured that had to be what my uncle had been up to."

McKay sat back rubbing at his thighs. That removed some of the mystery as to why their guide happened to know Dr. Morgenstern. He still wasn't sure he wanted to know all the details, though.

"What ever became of your uncle?"

She shrugged. "We see him on the res from time to time. Don't know what he's up to."

McKay frowned. He guessed she knew more than she was telling. He also realized she'd told him all she intended to. He'd been around the young woman enough to be aware how slim his chances of squirreling anything more out of her.

"What were you studying at the university?" he asked, just to be making conversation.

"Astrophysics." She stood up. "Come on, I think they got this *joto* about ready to go."

For what remained of the day they stayed in the eastern fringes of the Sierra Madre. The real mountains would put too uch strain on the fast-fading truck, and the low ground was able to be crawling with *Cristeros,* who could be expected to ke a lively interest in tourists from the atheistic USA even if ey didn't suspect them of being more than they appeared, so ey compromised.

When the sun started down Judy and Raúl put their heads gether. McKay had the impression initially that the two didn't ke each other too much. But since yesterday they'd mellowed the point of discussing the best place to lay up in Spanish.

The laager they picked was up a brushy draw well off the aved road they'd been following. "Not ideal," Judy comented, "but nothing is. Anywhere you go in this country, ou're laible to have people stumble across you at the weirdest our."

"Shit, you mean people *live* in this country?" Tandy said.

"You mean people *live* in Texas?"

He blinked. "Well, uh, I mean, it don't look as if anyone oes live around here."

"*Los Cristeros* forced many to leave," Raúl said, "but not veryone. Not up here."

So naturally Bill Warner had to be a big man. "We'll tell e sentries to off anybody comes across us," he said. "That ould take care of that."

"Billy," Rogers's voice said in McKay's ear. "That ain't ich a hot idea." Rogers was standing right there with his lips owing no more movement than an Olmec head's. He was iving his boss a subtle reminder without showing him up.

McKay nodded. "The hell with that. Anybody comes across , give him a couple of silver quarters and send him the hell n his way."

"Well, aren't you the sensitive soul, McKay? Such a liberal, nderstanding man." He gave a harsh laugh. "We'll have the icking Mexican Army crawling up our assholes in no time, e play it your way."

"You'll have 'em quicker if you go scragging the locals," udden Sam Coates offered, leaning with his elbow on a bat-red rear fender. "Or a mess of pissed-off friends and relations. his ain't the big city. People start wandering off and not oming back, somebody's going to come looking, sooner or ter."

"Shit, they'll probably reckon old Elfego's off on a drunk."

Coates nodded. "Maybe so, son. And maybe not. Reck⟨
we can take that chance?"

Warner turned away. His face looked almost purple und⟨
his red-clay tan. "Shit. You afraid of a bunch of half-ass⟨
indiges? We can kick their asses if they dick with us."

"What, you figure we ain't got problems enough that w
ought to pick fights all the way to Mexico City?" McKa
demanded.

"He's right, Bill," Richard Gallegos said quietly. Warn⟨
turned on him. It was the first time McKay had heard any ⟨
the squaddies contradict the corporal with the exception ⟨
Toliver. Warner looked at him for a moment, then turned ar
stomped off into the dusk.

The group broke up to attend to the various chores of makir
camp. McKay turned to find Judy Betzinez squatting on h⟨
heels a few meters up the slope chewing on a dry stalk of rabb⟨
grass.

"Dude's a small man in a big man's job," she remarke⟨
"He's going to do something to get somebody killed."

The military man's guild pride kicked in. McKay bristle⟨
"Look, he's got a tough job to do. Don't call for civilians ⟨
be second-guessing him."

She laughed. "Yeah. What do I know? I'm just a stup⟨
redskin."

Nobody came across them that night. But at dawn they a⟨
came awake at once with the familiar *thud-thud* of a dista⟨
.50-caliber machinegun pounding dully in their ears.

CHAPTER
FIFTEEN

McKay was out of his bedroll by the time he was fully conscious. Shiloh was running down the slope of the arroyo like a man wading through surf, raising a bow-wave of dust around the ankles of his boots, holding his machinegun by the carrying handle by one hand and his Kevlar Fritz helmet on his head with the other.

"Somebody's shootin'!" he called.

"Thanks, Shiloh, we never would've guessed that on our own." Toliver was up and moving with his rifle in his hands, old soldier to the core. Most of his young squadmates were glaring around looking for Charlie; he was halfway up the hill.

McKay followed him. At the top they saw nothing, just the Sierra Madre foothills tumbling downward to the plains. The .50-caliber shots sounded harder, clearer, and now they could hear the sound of small-arms fire like popcorn in a microwave.

McKay caught Toliver's eye and they both shook their heads. "We better check this out," McKay said. "Warner, leave a couple of men to look after the trucks. Gooding and Betzinez can stay back with them. Everybody else, saddle up and go."

The expected static from Warner about ordering him and his troopies around never materialized. Instead, here came Judy putting up the hill on her short but well-formed legs.

"Stay behind? Not on your life." She had her rifle slung over her back, an honest to Jesus Lee Enfield Mark V jungle carbine, slung muzzle down. Knowing whose niece she was McKay didn't doubt she could use it.

He hunched his shoulders in a quick its-your-funeral shrug. "Do you think that's a good idea, McKay?" Sloan's voice asked through his earphone. "Shouldn't we try to stay clear of trouble?"

"Negative," he subvocalized. "We do wanna stay out of trouble. But if there's a battle going on in the neighborhood, we need to know who and where."

Where was a rail line driving into the mountains from the east. *Who* was Mexican army regulars and a lot of *campesinos,* possibly *Cristeros,* possibly not, potting away at each other. It wasn't the peasants who had the .50s.

There was a train on the line, medium length to the eyes of Sam Sloan, who'd used to watch the trains highball past his swimming hole in the southeastern Missouri hills as a boy. Two diesel engines led it off, red and silver. It was blocked by a flatbed truck piled with rocks that had been parked across the tracks, a standard post-Holocaust roadblock up in the formerly United States, and a heap of trash including a couple of lengths of concrete conduit. The soldiers had .50 caliber M-2s mounted on several of the boxcars and were raking the surrounding hills with punishing fire.

The *campesinos* squatted behind boulders and bushes and blazed away with rifles. They weren't getting the better of the deal. When the thumb-sized slugs caught one they rolled him over the ground like a tumbleweed, or sometimes just tore him apart in a spray of blood visible from half a klick away.

"Lousy ambush," grunted Buck Toliver, lying on his belly on a hilltop with the others, taking it all in. "Coulda waited another couple miles, used dynamite to drop a bunch of boulders onto the line around a blind curve. Soldier boys woulda just plowed into it without a chance to react."

"Or just pried up the tracks," Judy Betzinez said.

Squatting just behind the crest with his M-16 grounded next to him, Raúl made a disparaging remark about residents of the state of Durango.

"Well, what the hell is going on?" McKay demanded around the stub of a cigar. The rope was unlit. In Indian country he wasn't about to send up wisps of smoke for bad guys to spot—or sniff.

"Hijacking, of course," Betzinez said. "And a damned poor one, like your friend says. Times are tough around here. Locals figure anything valuable enough to ship by train must be worth having. Not bad logic, except that means it's worth protecting, too."

Sam Sloan wondered about the level of poverty that would drive men to face .50-caliber machineguns with rifles; *he'd* seen what the things could do. Evidently he wasn't the only one wondering. The peasants decided to pack it in. They melted back into the hills, mostly staying low and using cover. A couple of them lost their heads, tossed down their guns and took off balls-out against the landscape. The MGs knocked down several, but the soldiers' hearts didn't seem to be in it.

As soon as the firing died, the train began to move forward again. The lead engine had a big snowplow-type blade fixed to the front of it. It began to shoulder the obstructions out of the way with a screeching metal-on-metal sound that went right through to the marrow of Sam's bones.

"Seen enough, McKay?" he asked.

McKay watched for a minute more, sheltering his eyes beneath a hand. "Affirmative." He slithered back from the crestline, dislodging a torrent of small pebbles. "Time to drive on."

They rolled across the line into Zacatecas, which was bordered to the east by San Luis Potosí, home state of *Hermana Luz*. They were coming into a region where they saw more people, fewer signs of destruction. They didn't need the taciturn Raúl to point out that was a bad sign: it was liable to signify an area that had submitted to the *Cristeros*, if not actually produced some.

They laagered in for the night in a cemetery tucked away out of sight of the nearest village behind a ridge. A few of the graves were marked with ornate marble headstones; the rest had little wooden crosses, some with plastic flowers nailed to them. Or nothing at all. Everybody made brittle cracks to show *they* weren't nervous about camping in a graveyard, except Judy Betzinez, who looked openly uncomfortable.

"The old ways die hard," she explained. "Maybe they shouldn't die at all, the way the world's gone. I know there's no ghosts, no such thing as corpse sickness. Still . . .'' She shrugged. All the same, she took her turn on watch, and slept soundly afterward.

The Guardians checked in with Morgenstern via satellite link. Actually, they made a call, and waited to be called back when the doctor was online.

"I can't believe it," Powell Gooding said as they huddled in their cold camp waiting for the annunciator chime. It was a cool night, with clouds blowing like patches of frayed cloth across the sky, and a hint of moisture in the wind. "I simply cannot *believe* that you would exclude Washington from your communications."

"Believe it," McKay said, gnawing a protein bar. It tasted like roofing tar. Some things never changed.

"But how can you be so paranoid?"

Sam Sloan laughed softly. "We were ambushed by the first person Washington sent us to make contact with, and after we let Washington know where we'd lit, the *Cristeros* were all over us like flies on a slice of jellied bread. Surely you can forgive us a touch of paranoia, Mr. Gooding?"

The diplomat shook his head impatiently. Before he could say anything a red light glowed alive on the satellite-link radio and a chime sounded softly. Sam pressed buttons, closing the connection and shutting out the speaker, so that only the Guardians could hear the transmission. Even he was unaware how high-handed that was.

"Guardians, do you read me?" a feminine voice said in their ears. "Guardians, respond please."

The Guardians drew a collective breath and then looked as one at Casey. He was very pale in the intermittent moonlight. The voice belonged to Angie Connoly, sometime lover of Casey's and daughter of none other than Maggie Connoly her own self. The last time they had heard that voice, it had been denouncing them for the murder of several inhabitants of the Freehold, the high-tech anarchist settlement in Colorado that had sheltered them several times in the past.

"Uh, this is the Guardians," Sam Sloan said after a moment. "We read you loud and clear. Go ahead please."

"This is the Freehold," Angie said unnecessarily. "We're helping maintain your communications net for this mission."

"Last time we heard from you you didn't seem to have such a high opinion of us, Ms. Connoly."

"Dr. Morgenstern gave us the whole story about the Liberators, Sam. We found enough evidence to corroborate what he told us." She paused. "Is Casey there?"

Sam's brown eyes flicked to the youthful-looking pilot. He sat twining his long, strong fingers like spiders trying the Kama Sutra. "That's affirmative, ma'am."

"Could I speak with him privately for a moment?"

Sloan glanced at McKay. Their leader shook his head. Casey's face fell, but then Sam realized McKay was just bemused.

"Go for it," McKay said.

"You got it," Sam said, and cut everyone out of the circuit but Case.

Whatever Angie and Casey said to each other, Casey was grinning like a jack-o'-lantern when Angie turned them over to Morgenstern. That was fortunate. The Israeli economist gave them little to smile about.

"It is absolutely imperative that you get to Mexico City as soon as possible," he said. "Sister Light has entered Mexico City and been welcomed, however grudgingly, by the provisional government."

"I thought they were bound and determined to keep her out, Doc," McKay said. "And I thought the squatters were doing it for them."

"They were. But apparently certain elements of the federal police attempted to move against the *Cristero* camp. They succeeded only in provoking a furious attack that led to heavy casualties among the squatters and allowed the *Cristeros* to force a route into the city. Once that happened, the provisional government bowed to the inevitable and requested a truce."

"Bummer," Casey remarked.

"Inarticulate but accurate, Lieutenant Wilson. Should the provisional government acquiesce further and accede her a role in government, that would be disastrous to us; in that event removing her could be as harmful as leaving her in place.

"That must not be permitted to happen."

Three hours after they hit the road next morning the truck sputtered and died. Casey and Richard investigated and said the distributor was history. They'd have to get a new one.

McKay sent Gallegos a few klicks on foot to the next village with Betzinez and Raúl and a pocket full of silver coins. The Chicano trooper knew what to look for, and the others could fill in if his border Spanish baffled the locals. All three seemed more than capable of looking out for themselves, which was fortunate, since McKay did not want to split up the Guardians right now.

Naturally, Powell Gooding sulked out loud; *he* was supposed to be handling the negotiations. Judy Betzinez laughed in his face.

"The fancy way you talk you're just going to piss people off," she told him. "*Nobody* lisps their C's and Z's in this country, except fools putting on airs pretending to be *gachupines*."

"*Gachupines?*" McKay asked.

"People born in Spain, Billy," Rogers explained.

As he should have guessed would happen, the stalled truck attracted a crowd. A horde of kids gathered round, staring in round-eyed interest at the truck. McKay made most of the party stay sweltering under canvas inside the vehicle near the weapons, letting only a couple out of any given moment, and then unarmed or with sidearms and concealed.

Tom Rogers got out and talked to the kids in Spanish, and soon had them laughing and gathering round for the hard candy he passed out—leave it to Tom to think of bringing that sort of thing, though it was sheer luck it had survived. But the adults drawn by the commotion hung back, their dark-eyed, almost Mongol faces solemn and unreadable.

"Shit," McKay said, "we got to ditch this truck. Nobody is gonna think we're tourists."

"Look on the bright side, man," Tandy suggested. "My man Richard don't turn up a new distributor, we be riding mules from here on in."

They occupied themselves playing poker in the airless rear of the captured Mexican truck. As one of their exercises before setting out on this pleasure spree, the 551st had blown open the vault of a derelict San Antonio bank. The pink and blue pre-war Federal Reserve notes were worth less even now than before the balloon went up, so the troopies carried them stuffed into their pockets by the handful and used them like Monopoly money.

"I see your hundred and raise you five hundred," Shig said with mock grimness, scattering a fistful of blue backs on an ammo crate.

"I call," Toliver drawled, lighting a cigar with a twenty. He held it up and watched it burn. "Shit. Too bad they did away with hundreds to screw up the drug dealers. Just ain't the same stokin' up with a measly double sawbuck."

"Mind you don't get ink on your fingers, there, Corporal," Tandy warned, folding his hand. "Hoo, this shit in my hand's worth less'n what I got in my pocket."

"My God," Powell Gooding said to McKay and Sloan, who were inside while Tom and Casey stretched their legs. "You call yourselves Guardians? How can you sit there and watch these men show disrespect for the government of the United States of America?"

"Since the day before the One-Day War a haircut cost me twenty-five bucks without even an appointment or some teeny-bopper with her boobs flopping around inside a sweatshirt rubbing goop in my hair, I'd say they're just callin' a spade a spade," McKay said.

"Are you trying to sow discord between us and our allies, Mr. Gooding?" Sloan asked sweetly. "Seems a funny occupation for a diplomat." Gooding sniffed and turned his face to the canvas wall.

Warner and the quiet Mexican kid Miguel sat alone with their thoughts, not participating in the grab-assing. Another sitting it out was DeWayne Burdick. He kept off by himself flipping a fat black beetle crawling across a crate onto its back with the tip of his Gerber combat knife and moodily watching it right itself.

His buddies had tried to get across to him that they didn't go along with Warner's notion he was to blame for Lucero's death, but they couldn't be too explicit without seeming to show disloyalty to their leader, and their *esprit* didn't permit them to do that. It was apparent that DeWayne bought Warner's jive complete with paper and string, at least to McKay. *Have to get Tom to talk to him about that,* he told himself. Things were getting too tight; a brooding trooper didn't concentrate, made mistakes. They couldn't afford that here and now.

As the party was beginning to get antsy in mid-afternoon, here came the foraging party, riding bicycles, for Jesus' sake. Richard and Judy were doubled up on a venerable Fuji mountain bike while Raúl labored along on a Schwinn one-speed that had to be older than McKay and maybe older than Sudden Sam. It had a basket hung on the bars with a bunch of greasy metal chunks in it.

"Where the hell did you get those?" McKay said, pointing at the bikes with his chin as the party dismounted.

"Bought them in town with the rest of the parts," Richard said, "Didn't cost much."

"Figured we were on a tight schedule, so we should get back as soon as possible," Betzinez said. "You invading Mexico on an expense account?"

McKay glanced back at Gooding, who had his mouth pursed into an expression of disapproval. Or maybe that was its rest state. "What's your damn hurry? I thought you Indians had no sense of time."

He heard Sloan's breath hiss between his teeth. Judy laughed.

"We don't."

"But then, why—" He shook his head. "Never mind. Just never mind."

Richard and Casey got the new piece slapped in in record time and in a matter of minutes they were crawling onto the pavement again in a shower of gravel that sent the laughing, waving crowd of kids scattering. Looking back over the tailgate McKay saw some more adults just watching them. He didn't like the looks of that, but there was jack they could do about it; no matter what Corporal Bill's tattoo said, you *couldn't* kill 'em all.

They still had a healthy chunk of daylight left when they found their way back in the heights, undulating along the face of a fairly steep range of hills. They were hitting a lot of traffic now, as if the *Cristero* uprising had never happened — as if the Third World War had never happened.

"Now I know what they were talking about when they said people drove like maniacs down here," Sam Sloan said. He and McKay were riding back by the tailgate watching the cars and trucks howl past their laboring deuce-and-a-half. "They're zipping by as if this were a superhighway straight down the middle of Kansas, instead of a two-lane road along a thousand foot cliff."

McKay glanced back. A bus was closing rapidly from behind. It had a tone of luggage strapped onto the racks up top, including a coop full of chickens. There was a huge portrait of the Virgin Mary taped in front of the rearview mirror — McKay had finally quit wincing every time he saw that painting, once Raúl and Sudden Sam explained it didn't mean anything, *everyone* in Mexico was a fan of the Virgin of Guadalupe, not just the *Cristeros*.

"I know what you mean. But have faith. We got Casey at the wheel." He was up there yakking away with Richard Gallegos. A shared affinity for vehicles had made the two instant friends for life.

Sloan shuddered. "That's what worries me. *He'd* drive like that, if he could."

He gestured out the back of the truck as the bus swerved into the other lane, horn blaring. McKay caught a glimpse of a pair of blurred young faces as the deuce-and-a-half rocked slightly in the backwash, heavy-laden though it was.

"Jesus Christ!" he exclaimed. "There's a couple of *campesinos* riding on the rear bumper of that thing."

Then a pickup truckload of peasants coming back from market rolled around the curve just ahead. The bus smacked into it head-on, spinning it around. Then both vehicles just took right on off into space.

CHAPTER
SIXTEEN ————————————

Instinctively Casey ditched to the right. McKay was already in motion, vaulting over the tailgate with Sloan right behind.

The bus hit once, bounced, and blew up. It arced to the bottom of the cliff blazing like a comet. The pickup went down beside it spinning end for end, spilling people and pigs and chickens and baskets.

"They're not supposed to blow up like that except in the movies," Sloan said, peering over the edge. His rectangular James Garner face was very pale.

"Gas tank might not've needed much to pop it," Sudden Sam said from beside him. "Or maybe somebody had a big can of kerosene aboard. Happens sometimes."

Three hundred meters below the bus blazed merrily in a ravine. The truck lay not far from it, not looking much like a truck anymore. All around the Guardians people were pulling over to the side and getting out to grab each others' arms and point excitedly down into the flamelit shadows.

One of the men who'd been riding on the bus's rear bumper was sitting on the road on his ass, staring around bewilderedly.

He got to his feet and began to walk unsteadily up the road.

"Shouldn't we do something to help?" Sloan asked.

McKay stirred an unlit cigar butt around in his mouth. "Nothin' we can do. And we got an appointment to keep in Mexico." He'd started to pick up the local habit of referring to the capital that way and dropping the *City*.

He turned and started back to the truck. Powell Gooding grabbed his arm. His eyes stood out wildly from a white face. "My God, how can you walk away from those people? We have to do something!"

Sudden Sam Coates leaned out over the unrailed cliff to peer down. "McKay's right. Nobody survived that. No way to help them if they had."

"Are you dead to all compassion? Have you no human feelings? Good Lord, this is a major disaster! There must be fifty people on that bus."

"More likely a hundred," Coates said. "They pack 'em in down here."

Gooding turned around to the crowd of motorists, who weren't showing signs of trying to help. "What's the matter with you? Why isn't anybody doing anything?"

"This is Mexico," Raúl said.

"Hey! Look down there." The 551st squaddies had deassed the truck, as much to stretch their legs and breathe fresh air as to see what was going on. DeWayne Burdick was pointing ahead and downward.

An arroyo that might have been cut into the mountainside with a giant axe transversed the road about thirty meters ahead of where the truck was parked. A short bridge crossed it on a framework of girders. The bus had been about to go over it when it hit the pickup.

A little girl in a pink dress sat on the ground beside the cement footing of one of the upright girders. Her hair had been wound around two narrow paper cones on the front of her head, giving her the appearance of having horns. She was crying.

Before anyone could react Burdick had plunged off the road and was skating down the slope toward her, slowing himself by grabbing at clumps of brush.

"Jesus, what's he think he's doing?" McKay asked.

The footing was sunk next to a ten-foot slab of red sandstone, absolutely vertical. The only way for Burdick to reach her was to shinny down that. The soil to either side was too loose and treacherous; one step onto that would have sent him all the way down.

He dropped beside her, barely stopped himself from sliding away by a quick snatch at the girder. He put an arm around her, comforting her, then stood up.

Powell Gooding had gone right behind him. He was perched atop the sandstone slab, hand outstretched to the trooper.

"Aw, fuck *me*," McKay said. He started forward to lend a hand. Gooding's racquetball muscle was never going to be enough to hoist the husky Burdick and the little girl from such precarious footing.

But Gooding wasn't waiting. Burdick stepped up on a low jut and reached up to take hold of his hand. The diplomat set his jaw and pulled.

Starting over the lip with his heart in his throat McKay heard a soft thump and a grunt from Burdick. The trooper's body jerked.

His hand opened.

With a scream he fell away. Gooding clutched madly after him. McKay only stopped him from going over the edge by diving forward and seizing a handful of checked Pendleton shirt as Burdick and the girl pinwheeled down into the ravine. The child's pink skirts billowed out like a parasol as she fell.

The sound of a shot reached McKay's ears. His head cranked left, lips drawn into a snarl around his cigar. Where the highway bellied out around another hill four hundred meters behind there were uniformed men on horseback in the road, and several dismounted men kneeling, pointing rifles their way.

"*Montañeros!*" Raúl shouted. At the instant Burdick was hit Shiloh had dived into the truck. Now he popped up and slammed the M-249 down across the tailgate, his one eye glaring furiously as he let a whole magazine go.

Bullets kicked up spouts of dirt around McKay as he hauled Gooding bodily back up the near-vertical slope. Judy Betzinez dropped to one knee, bringing the Limey jungle carbine to her shoulder. She fired. A horse reared and went over the edge, shrill screams of animal and man blending as they tumbled down the cliff face in a vortex of dirt.

In the shock of watching the collision everybody except the Chiricahua woman had piled out without any weapons but sidearms, which were worth exactly zip at this range. There was a mad scramble to get back into the deuce-and-a-half and get hands on hardware. Meanwhile McKay was scrambling over the top, listening to deep whines as bullets ricocheted past his ears. Those were 7.62 slugs they were firing at him. A solid hit anywhere would send him spinning down to join Burdick and the hapless passengers of the wrecked vehicles. He hurled Gooding past him onto the pavement and scrabbled toward the truck on all fours like a big lizard.

The excited onlookers had simply disappeared. He and Gooding and Betzinez were all alone out there on the pavement as a bunch of mean Indians blazed away at them with FNs.

As he reached the truck the muzzle of a grenade launcher stuck out almost in his face, looking big enough to crawl down. He ducked as the weapon burped a grenade at the mounted policemen. Then hands were hauling him and the others aboard as Casey put the pedal to the metal and wheels spun on gravel.

A round cracked harmlessly through the canvas overhead as he rolled over and landed heavily on a tarp-covered mound of supplies. He sat up and looked back. A cloud of teargas was dissipating rapidly in the brisk breeze. The tough *federales* were still firing, seemingly unaffected by it, though he saw a couple of shapes lying still or kicking on the asphalt. Everybody was sitting on top of his Maremont. He felt like hauling out his .45 and busting a few caps at them like George C. Scott firing his six-shooter at the Heinkels in *Patton*.

Then they were around the lethal bend and out of the line of fire. For the moment.

"This is where I leave you," Judy Betzinez said. She was standing next to a six-lane highway with the wind whipping the feather in her hatband. She wasn't exactly what McKay would call a pretty woman, but she was attractive, and she looked damned cute standing there in the early-morning sun.

"Sure you won't reconsider?" Sam Sloan asked, showing her his best hillbilly grin. "You've been a powerful help to us so far."

A semi hurtled past like an avalanche in progress. Sam

ducked his head in response, then looked sheepishly around, only to see his comrades doing the same thing. There was a lot of traffic on this brand-new highway above the city of Zacatecas, more than ever giving the impression World War III had just been a bad dream. It was like paying a visit to another world.

She shook her head firmly. "I've done what I set out to do: worked out a way to get you safely to Mexico City. Now I'm gone."

He turned around and looked a their "safe passage" to the capital. "If you say so," he said dubiously.

It was a semitrailer rig. The tractor was streamlined, gleaming black. The name EL PIPIRIBAU was picked out in reflective studs on the front bumper, beneath a sheet-metal silhouette of a reclining naked woman spot-welded to the grille and next to a sticker that read Yo (heart) Chihuahua. Flowers were painted on the enameled sides. The edges of hood, cab, and the sleeping compartment were outlined by little blinky lights. The raked windscreen was about one-quarter obscured by stickers representing the Virgin of Guadalupe, Juan Diego displaying his robe with the miraculous image of the Virgin of Guadalupe, Jesus holding open his robe to display his Sacred Heart, and Merith Tobias in the nude. Standing with one split-soled cowboy boot up on the running board was the owner and operator of this magnificent vehicle, a rake-thin youth with a prominent Adam's apple, a missing front tooth, and a cowboy hat, who wanted to be called Johnny.

"It's a lot less conspicuous than the deuce-and-a-half, Sam," Tom Rogers said, noticing his expression.

"If you say so."

"It'll get you into Mexico in one straight shot. You ride in the back where no one can get curious about what a bunch of *gringos* is up to. It'll work fine."

Johnny nodded his head in enthusiastic agreement with what she was saying, in spite of the fact that he neither spoke nor understood English.

They'd spent the night with some distant relatives of Raúl's who lived forty klicks northeast of Zacatecas. Raúl and Judy had gone off to promote some new means of transportation.

The truck was dying on them, and was pretty thoroughly compromised by now anyway.

During the night the radio had chimed for attention. Dr. Morgenstern was on the line with late-breaking news: the provisional government had agreed to admit *Hermana Luz* to its ranks. The formal ceremony was scheduled for three days from the coming morning, in the *Zócalo*.

It was up to the Guardians to see that it never took place.

A couple of hours later the intrepid scouts returned to announce they'd gotten everything arranged.

Everybody piled into the trailer on top of the gear, which was smothered with tarps to keep it from shifting as much as possible. The exception was McKay. Judy Betzinez got him settled in riding shotgun with Johnny in the cab, his Maremont M-60E3 between his knees, and stood on the running board with a half-smile on.

"So, I guess this is it."

"Yeah." He chewed his lower lip. "Say, are you sure you'll be all right and everything?"

She laughed. "I can take care of myself. The question is, will *you* be all right? I've spent most of my time looking after you people, in case you didn't notice."

"Uh. Yeah. We get to Mexico, we can do the job."

She leaned forward suddenly and kissed his cheek. Then she hopped to the ground.

"So long, McKay. You're not a bad guy, for a white-eyes."

"Thanks."

Johnny grinned and engaged the gears. The semi pulled into the traffic stream. McKay watched Judy Betzinez in the wing mirror. As soon as the big truck was underway she turned and started walking along the highway in the opposite direction. She got smaller and smaller, and then was gone.

Johnny drove like everyone else in Mexico, and kept his stereo system cranked up all the way. He must have had a hundred watts per channel in that damned cab; McKay was sure he'd be having *mariachi* aftershocks in his skull for a week, in case he survived the ride. He wondered long and hard if it was such a good idea to insist on riding up front. *Shoulda made Tom do it,* he told himself. *He's the specialist in keeping an eye on the indiges.*

But they made it to Mexico City without incident, past what looked like miles of lunar landscape with little tarpaper and cardboard shacks dotted across it, squatters' shanties, showing slivers of light through makeshift blackout curtains, into the largest city that remained in the world.

Well after dark the truck pulled into the cracked and weed-grown lot of an ice factory closed down by the government as part of a water-rationing program. Young Miguel was related to somebody who'd worked there; he knew the place was abandoned, and was able to give Johnny instructions on how to find it. McKay was beginning to realize that everyone in Mexico was related to somebody who knew anyone you cared to name in the goddam country.

The plant was padlocked. A hefty crowbar from El Pipiribau's tool locker took quick care of that. Tom offered the perpetually grinning Johnny the rest of his payment, in gold, and appropriate flowery words of thanks, as the others unloaded their equipment and carried it inside.

Sam stood watching the little lights twinkling around the tractor's silhouette and shook his head. "What a country."

"Hey, don't knock it," McKay said. "I think I'll get a truck and fix it up just like that, if this hitch ever ends."

"You're hopeless, McKay."

"You got that right."

CHAPTER
SEVENTEEN ─────────

McKay took off for a reconnaissance the next morning. Tom, Richard Gallegos, Raúl, and Sudden Sam Coates went along, all got up in their horrible tourist clothes those fucking Indians had saddled them with. In spite of himself, McKay found himself liking and respecting the Texas Ranger captain; he was a capable hand, with a keen eye and a good set of wits. Also, he spoke the lingo and knew the country, which was more than McKay could say.

He took Raúl because Raúl was their guide, after all—McKay didn't put much stock in the kid Miguel, even if he had turned up the ice plant for them. Gallegos came because he spoke Spanish and could pass for a local at a glance and was good troop, and also it would piss the Texicans off mightily if they were left out, especially since Sudden Sam was going. Tom Rogers was along because he spoke Spanish and knew everything.

The ever-capable Rogers hot-wired a handy Toyota. They squeezed inside and set out through the congestion in the streets of the Federal District, which was incredible despite a bewildering array of regulations and restrictions attempting to limit the use of private vehicles. Canny Mexicans dealt with them the way they dealt with any government edicts they found inconvenient: they ignored them.

McKay was less than ecstatic about traveling around in daylight with everyone in the goddam country on the lookout for them, in person. But Raúl assured him there'd be no problem. *Gringos* were not particularly conspicuous in the capital, even in the wake of the One-Day War. There were plenty of expatriate Americans and Canadians and whatnot, and even a fair number of tourists from the Federated States of Europe, which blew McKay's mind. McKay worried anyway.

But there was no way in hell they were going to figure out a way to pop the nations' number one celebrity sometime in the next three days by lying low in the ice factory. Time to bite the bullet.

"Find anything?" McKay asked when they rendezvoused back by the car in late afternoon. They'd split up, with Tom going off with Coates, and McKay teamed with Richard Gallegos, while Raúl drifted around on his own to see what he could pick up.

Tom nodded. "Let's talk while we drive. Traffic gets even worse around here in another hour or so. Rush hour."

Gallegos appropriated the wheel. McKay got in the passenger seat, leaving the others to squeeze into the back. As big as he was, McKay wasn't folding himself into the back of a riceburner.

They were tossing around facts and impressions when they heard a tinny little *weeble-weeble* siren behind them. Everybody looked in the rearview mirror to see flashing blue lights and an ancient blue and white Volkswagen beetle, of all things, hanging on their bumper.

"Shit, Richard, what did you do?" McKay demanded.

"I didn't do nothin'; it's a shakedown." He pulled over the side of the street, eyes switching nervously between mirror and traffic.

They were pulled over by a little park with a little cement fountain and a lot of vendors parked under some straggly trees. McKay was startled to see a small, square woman in a blue uniform jacket and white turtleneck, black hair pulled into a severe bun beneath a billed cap, appear in the window, notebook in one white-glove hand.

"*Transita*," Raúl explained. "Woman, how you say, traffic cop."

"Great," McKay said. Richard was swiveling his head left and right now, giving explanations in alternate English and Spanish of how he'd done nothing wrong.

Whether he had or whether they were having the bite put on them all at once became academic. The *transita* leaned down to peer into the car and looked Billy McKay in the eye. Her head kind of recoiled back inside her turtleneck, and her sleepy eyes got wide. She started spilling syllables from her mouth. McKay caught the words *los guardianes,* and his heart dropped right on into his poorly fitting sneakers.

Sitting between Coates and Raúl, Tom Rogers brought up his left hand. In it he held his .45 with a fat silencer screwed on the end of the barrel. He fired past Richard's left ear. The shot hit the *transita* above her right eyebrow. Her head snapped back as the rear of her cranium blew out and she dropped straight down to the pavement.

"*Shit!*" Richard screamed. A few drops of blood had splashed back and hit him in the face. But he had the presence of mind to pop the clutch and get them the hell out of there.

McKay turned around in his seat. He hadn't noticed Rogers screwing the silencer onto his piece, didn't even know he had it along. Behind them, a couple of vendors stood looking down at the sprawled traffic cop. Nobody was paying them any attention at all.

Thank God for Tom Rogers, he thought. It was time to think of more insurance. Maybe they'd used up their bad luck on this mission—they'd had more than their share of it, for sure. But he was never going to bet on a proposition like that.

"We got to make a slight detour on the way back to the ice plant," he said.

"Sister Light is staying *here,*" McKay said, stabbing his forefinger at a map spread out on a crude wooden table in the loading area of the defunct plant. It wasn't the fancy Defense Intelligence Agency map they'd been packed off from Texas with. That had gone up in smoke during the ambush in

Chihuahua. It was a city map Richard had swiped from a Pemex station, while McKay was haggling with the attendant about what it would cost him to get the key to go take a leak.

He tapped a spot not far from the *Zócalo*. "They got her set up in some sort of old villa, used to belong to a rich Basque family. It's the damnedest thing for the middle of a big city: great big grounds, couple acres at least, big trees, all kinds of fancy vines and shrubs and shit." His words echoed through the high-ceilinged cinder-block structure, chasing each other like rats in and around and through the tangle of tanks and pipes and catwalks and coils.

The 551st squaddies showed their teeth in the twilight filtering through yellowed windows covered with green-painted metal mesh set high in the walls. "Ain't that a pity," Tandy said. He was sharpening a huge Bowie-pattern knife on a flat stone. "All that good ground cover. Shoot, don't they want this to be a challenge?"

McKay half-grinned. "Well, the joint's surrounded by four-meter walls topped with broken glass."

"Piece of cake," Shiloh said. He was dabbing at a strip of cloth with cammie-paint sticks, trying to work a way to camouflage his bandages.

"And the grounds're crawling with *Cristeros*." The squaddies shared a look at that and never even answered. "Also, there's a squad of regulars supported by a machinegun jeep. Finally, they got these goons in suits, Panama hats, and windsurfing shades hanging around. Dunno who they are. Look like basic Third World secret pigs."

Raúl muttered briefly to Rogers, then said, "Federal Security Directorate. They are how you called them."

"Yo. They got some kind of fancy little machine pistols in shoulder holsters, mini-Uzis or something like that. Those dudes come and go, so we don't know how many there are." He grimaced. "We couldn't hang around all that long. Even Third World cops are going to notice when a blond *gringo* in a fucking aloha shirt who's twice as big as anybody else in sight spends the whole afternoon hanging out watching a security zone."

"After dark we'll go have a look at it," Warner said. McKay hesitated a fraction of a second, then nodded. Warner was a jerk and too emotionally unstable for this job, but he knew his stuff.

"Right. But right now, let's eat. I'm starving."

"Man," Richard said, stuffing his mouth with fancy Lurps rations, "you should've seen the look on this poor bitch's face. She was just about to blow our cover all over the street, and *pow!* Tommy pops her. Right between the eyes. Damn bullet about nicked my ear, man. Damn."

Sam choked and set his messkit down on the pitted cement floor. "You killed a policewoman?"

"A *transita*," Richard said. "Lady traffic cop. Had to do it, man. She recognized us somehow."

"Sunday supplements had articles on us down here, just like in the States, I guess," McKay said.

"Don't you think it was a bit conspicuous to just shoot her in broad daylight?" Sloan said.

"Sloan, get real," McKay said, feeling his neck get warm. "The whole fucking country is looking for us. We're evil invaders from the north. Everybody automatically hates us, all right? She could fuck us over royal just reporting back what she'd seen. But she was getting ready to start yelling about us then and there. We might have had the whole street on top of us."

"And—shooting her didn't get everyone after you?" From the hitch in his voice it was clear he'd been tempted to use stronger language. But you didn't just take off and accuse a buddy of cold-blooded murder. Especially since it was Tommy, who didn't make mistakes; Sloan had to know he'd done the right thing. But his liberal sensibilities were outraged. He had to blow off some steam.

"Pistol was silenced, man," Richard said. "Nobody heard anything. For all they knew, we just pushed her."

"Police are not very popular," Raúl said. "Even traffic girls."

Gooding stood up, dumping his own dinner to the cement. "I can't believe I'm hearing this. You people are discussing murder in cold blood as if it's going for a ride in the country."

Buck Toliver looked up at him from beneath his shock of straw-colored hair. "What the fuck did you think we came down here for, Powell? We're supposed to off a teenage girl.

Don't that stick in your craw?"

Powell threw up his arms and stomped off into the shadows.
There were plenty of them; the little kerosene lantern Johnny
had left with them didn't offer much in the way of light.

Warner stood up. "Fuck this. Let's go scope out our objec-
tive."

"You got it," McKay said.

"Whoo-ee, will you look at *that*," Warner said.

From what Mckay knew or thought he knew about Mexico
the swarms of workmen hammering together a big speaker's
platform in the middle of the *Zócalo* long after dark was a
pretty unusual sight. But it was the big sheet of blackness they
were erecting against the almost self-luminous haze of the nighttime sky that Warner was pointing to.

"What the hell is it?" McKay asked.

"Diamondvision screen," said Tom. "Big old TV, like they
got in stadiums to show replays."

"Son of a bitch."

Tom stopped a pedestrian going past with hands stuck in the
pockets of a tan windbreaker, though the night was quite warm.
"He says it's for the big ceremony for *Hermana Luz*," he said
after some rapid Spanish. "They want the multitudes to be able
to see the Little Virgin's holy face clearly." From the way the
Mexican spat as Rogers spoke, McKay got the idea he was
maybe not a big fan of the prophetess from San Luis Potosí.

"Ask him what he thinks of this."

Rogers looked at McKay a moment with his impassive gray
eyes, then spoke quietly to the man.

"He says it sucks."

They didn't learn a whole lot more from snooping and poop-
ing around *Hermana Luz's* palace than they already knew. It
was a three-story affair with whitewashed walls and a pitched
roof of red tiles shaped like cylinders sawed in half lengthwise.
It had a big fancy veranda with vines of some sort climbing
up the pillars. There were little wrought-iron balconies hung
outside the windows on the upper floors.

There were probably a hundred armed *Cristeros* wandering
around the grounds, and every once in a while the FN-MAG

mounted jeep putted out the big wrought-iron gates to take a turn around the block to impress would-be evil-doers. The would-be evil-doers were not impressed.

The lights blazed all over the mansion until about two in the morning. "Shit, this chick must have a pretty hard-core social life for a virgin," Warner remarked from the rooftop of the apartment building across the street when the lights finally started to go out.

"Probably holding strategy meetings, that kind of crap," McKay said.

They crept back down the stairs inside the apartment. From the afternoon's reconnaissance they knew the place was packed with *Cristeros*. All three of them were armed with silenced sidearms, though, so they weren't too worried.

Nobody made the mistake of sticking his head out or coming back from a bender. They reached the street without incident and went off in search of a likely car to boost.

They left the car in a warehouse district a few blocks from the ice plant. "Makes me homesick," McKay muttered, thinking of youthful exploits in Pittsburgh's inner city as they wandered home through streets redolent of *mariachi* music and toasting cheese.

Warner laughed quietly. "Don't it, though? I remember one time in Pampa, up in the Panhandle, the night we whipped the Dumas Demons in a big game. We got liquored up and swiped the chief of police son's car. Studly sumbitch; Porsche Turbo 944. 'Course, we married that sucker to a power pole. Had to get twenty-five stitches in my scalp, and that was the easy part, compared to what Chief Hillerman did to me when he got his hands on me."

McKay glanced at him. He'd been all professional and not one bit of bullshit tonight. Bastard kept that up, McKay was in danger of starting to like him.

The ice plant looked even darker and more deserted than when they left. "Shit," Warner said, "didn't those idiots leave anybody on watch?" He pushed open the chipped green metal door.

McKay heard a crunch of grit beneath leather behind him. The hairs on the back of his bull neck were already on the rise;

he put a hand on the Pachmayr grips of the pistol stuck in his waistband and started to turn.

Tom Rogers's hand on his arm stopped him dead. "*Don't, Billy,*" he subvocalized. "*Too late.*"

With agonized slowness McKay turned.

Four men in linen suits, Panama hats, and sunglasses stood in a semicircle behind them, covering them with Uzis.

CHAPTER
EIGHTEEN

"*My fault, Billy,*" Tom subvocalized as the men in the hats and dark glasses prodded them through the door with the stub barrels of their submachine guns. "*I should've smelled them.*"

He meant it, too; now that McKay's attention was called to it he caught a faint whiff of some sort of cologne or aftershave, and he knew Rogers's nose was much more sensitive than his.

A match flared, briefly illuminating a lean face with knife-edge sideburns. A cigarette glowed. The ember drifted like a firefly down to the wick of the kerosene lamp.

"So you are the Guardians," said the man with the sideburns as he turned the light up high. "I can't tell you how proud I am to meet you." He gave a shark's grin. "Especially under the circumstances." His English was immaculate as the white French cuffs of his shirt.

"Looks to me like you've met a couple of us already," McKay said grimly. Casey and Sam sat next to a compressor with their hands strapped behind them. A pair of goons in suits stood right next to them with Czech-made Skorpion machine pistols pressed to their temples. "Are you two all right?"

"Except for our pride," Sloan said. He had a purplish bruise on one cheek that made a liar out of him. Casey looked unhurt but furious.

The 551st troopies and the two Mexican guides sat apart, also under guard. Their arms were strapped behind them with nylon restraints. Secret cops hustled over to immobilize the newcomers' arms the same way.

"Ah, yes. But not the famed William McKay, leader of the Guardians. Or his illustrious comrade Thomas Rogers. Some of my Sandinista colleagues would be even more pleased than I to make your acquaintance, Lieutenant Rogers."

"Thought you folks didn't get along too well with Nicaraguans, after they tried to invade," McKay said, trying not to wince as the restraints were snugged tight around his forearms.

"But of course they did us a very large favor, allowing us to unify the country in a moment of great peril. Besides, I understand you have a background in covert operations. You should know that in the world of intelligence and counterintelligence there are no permanent enemies." He puffed his cigarette. "Or permanent friends."

"How the hell do you know all this about us?" McKay demanded.

"By fascinating coincidence certain members of *Hermana Luz*'s entourage possess very extensive information about you."

"Vesensky."

The secret policeman cocked an eyebrow. "Is that his name? Very interesting. They have been at pains to conceal his identity from us, though of course that's fruitless. You shall have to tell me about this Vesensky. We have so much to talk about." The cigarette traced a smoke arabesque in air. "But I forget my manners. I am *Coronel* Bustamante. Of the Federal Security Directorate—but surely you've guessed that."

Tom Rogers said something quick in Spanish. Bustamante's face turned several shades darker. He recovered quickly, and laughed. "A noble effort, Lieutenant. But your situation is hopeless, so attempting to provoke me won't serve you at all." His expression hardened. "And saying things for which you can be made to pay is hardly prudent, don't you think, my friend? Get them out to the van."

At a jerk of his head the secret policemen began to hustle

the captives to their feet. As he was being pulled toward the door Bill Warner suddenly jerked free. "Coates!" he screamed. "Where's Coates? That motherfucking Ranger's gone. *He's sold us out!*"

Bustamante's hand snaked inside his coat and came out with a Skorpion. "*¡Hay un otro!*" he shouted, and McKay had absorbed enough Spanish to realize that meant *there's another*. McKay thought he'd confused Warner's meaning.

But Bustamante was a veteran of the dreaded White Brigade and Mexico's "dirty war" against its terrorists; his instincts were good. Something the size and shape of a tin can dropped down from the blackness above the hemisphere of lamplight and bounced on the cement two meters in front of McKay.

Everything snapped into slow-motion. McKay dropped by reflex. Already he knew just exactly what was about to happen with sick certainty.

He shut his eyes as the cement hit him hard. Just on general principles.

The stun grenade cracked off, deafening McKay for the moment. Had his eyes been open it would have dazzled him, filling his eyes with big basketballs of light for seconds, seconds that could be crucial in a firefight. That was why the stun bombs were such useful little items.

But even though it was the middle of the night Bustamante and his boys, *macho* men that they were, were wearing *sunglasses*. And that blocked most of the dazzling effect of the grenade.

Up on the catwalk Sudden Sam Coates cursed as the colonel stepped behind a hunk of machinery. He shifted aim and fired a burst from his tommy gun at two men with Uzis who were standing there flatfooted, not stunned but stupid. They went down in a spray of blood.

Another cop whipped out his tiny machine pistol and fired a burst at chest level. Miguel screamed as bullets lanced through him. Too late Coates chopped the Skorpion gunner down.

It was all shot to hell. He'd hoped to give the boys a chance to break for it, but that was blown—those dumb secessionist bastards were the only ones his bomb *had* stunned. He saw Bustamante drawing a bead on him, tried to haul the M-1A1 around, knowing he had no time.

The muzzle blast of the Skorpion looked like a volcanic explosion. Coates felt impacts in his chest and right arm. He still tried to bring the SMG to bear on the secret policeman, but he had no strength in his arms. His chest was a vast black sea, and as his knees gave way the blackness flooded over him.

McKay winced as the old Ranger flopped on the cement three meters away from him. The Security Directorate goons were busting caps all over hell. Bullets were whizzing everywhere, bouncing off the floor and the icemaking equipment, whining and buzzing like yellowjackets.

Over it all he heard Bustamante screaming, and he didn't have to know Spanish to know the colonel was ordering everyone to cease fire right now or he was going to kick ass and take names. A country full of Keystone Kops and they had to get busted by a hardcase who knew his job.

The firestorm stopped. The captives were herded out to a van with windows covered by metal mesh while a couple of police wounded by friendly fire were tended to. They dragged Miguel out by his hair.

He bled to death before their eyes on the way to the FSD headquarters. The metal floorboards were awash in blood when the doors were hauled open and the prisoners were ordered out into the night.

"Now," the unseen interpreter said, "why don't you tell us why you have come here."

Billy McKay was stark naked and strapped to a chair with his arms cinched painfully tight behind its straight back. His balls hung onto the cool wood of the seat. The chief interrogator sat at the table across from McKay in a little spill of light from a desk lamp, smiling all across his Frankenstein face.

With a certain amount of effort McKay raised his head. He'd been worked over preparatory to being tied down. One eye was swollen half shut and his head was pounding. His nose might be broken, too, which wasn't a new experience for him. The beating had been reassuring in a way; it was an amateur stunt, not something men who knew what they were doing would do, at least not to somebody like McKay. Little men showing how big they were, essentially harmless, though hav-

ng people hit you in the head was never going to be a hundred
percent risk free. Then the big boss came in with his merry
crew and McKay started to get concerned.

"You people seem to know all the answers already." His
mouth was numb, as if he'd been doing coke all night. "What
do you need me for?"

The translator translated. The man with the huge ugly head
murmured back. "We wish to have our information confirmed.
Now, please make life easier for all of us and talk."

"Go fuck yourself."

The vast head nodded. The totally hairless man who sat
beside him turned a rheostat, sending an electric current from
the alligator clamp fastened to the head of McKay's penis to
the other contact clamped to the base of his scrotum.

McKay screamed.

He pulled in three huge sobbing breaths. "You ain't gonna
get anything out of me like this, you know," he managed to say.

"Perhaps not," the interrogator said through his interpreter.
"But this pastime affords great pleasure to Roldán, here"—he
waved a hand at the hairless man, who looked like Freddy
Krueger's ugly brother—" and he has few amusements in life.

"So: why have you invaded Mexico?"

McKay moistened cracked lips, tasted blood. *Something tells
me this isn't gonna be much fun.*

Slowly consciousness came back. Then without warning it
was pounding like the hooves of a stampeding herd of cattle
inside his head. He moaned.

"Welcome back to the land of the living," he heard Buck
Toliver rasp. "For now, anyway."

He was aware of the cool hardness of cement along the single
great bruise that was his body, but the back of his head was
resting on something soft by comparison. He worked at an eye
glued shut by dried blood and found himself looking up into
the concerned face of Sam Sloan, in whose lap his head was
resting. Sam quickly looked away, self-conscious.

"Thanks, Sloan, but I can take it from here." He sat up
rubbing the back of his head. His brain and stomach did an
Immelmann in perfect synchronization and he lay back down
again. "No, I guess I won't. Jesus, my dick hurts."

"We took a look at it, which shows you the kind of sacrifice we make for comrades in arms," Toliver said. "We don't think it's gonna have to come off."

He turned his head and made both eyes open. The room was about five meters square, with windowless green-painted walls and a bare cement floor that sloped inward to a single drain. There was no furniture except a dented bucket in the corner.

"Lucky we're in this here special ultra-modern detention facility insteada one of them Mexican jails, huh?" Tandy said.

The only other person in the room was Raúl, sitting against the wall with his knees pulled up to his chin. "Where are the others?"

"We think they're in another tank, McKay," Sloan said.

"What about Gooding? Seen any sign of him?"

"No. We hope he got clean away."

"Jesus." That would be too much to take, for all these elite warriors to get trapped like birds in a net, while that cookie-pushing son of a bitch managed to escape.

"Maybe he can complain to the U.S. embassy," Toliver said, and laughed.

"So what happens now?" Sloan asked, pushing back the silence that had started to crowd the cramped cell.

"The cavalry rides in and rescues us," McKay said. "Barring that, we come up with one hell of a plan on short notice. Any ideas?"

"You got me," Tandy admitted. Raúl smiled sadly and shook his head.

"Then that means we're gonna have to improvise."

Their captors had taken their watches, and they couldn't see sunlight, if there was any to be seen. Without reference to the outside world time passed at its own pace. It gave them something to argue about, to take their minds off the hopelessness.

Sometime later—McKay thought it was 1400, Toliver judged it after 1700, and Tandy insisted it was still morning—the cell door banged open. Warner came flying in and landed in a heap in the center of the floor, where he lay face down and sobbing.

Sitting with his back to the wall, McKay tried to get up. "What the fuck—?"

"Save your breath, *gringo*," said one of the men at the door. "Save all of it. He told us all we wanted to know." Laughing, he slammed the door.

In the sudden silence the sound of bolts being thrown was loud as a punch press.

Toliver knelt by his commander's side. "Bill, are you all right?"

Feebly Warner batted his hand away. "I did it," he sobbed. "I told them. Everything."

"Hey, take it easy," Toliver said, embarrassed.

"They put me in a room and tied me to a chair," Warner said into his forearms. "They asked me questions. I told them to go take a running jump. So they brought in Shiloh, and they made him kneel right in front of me, and that bastard Bustamante put a gun in his ear and blew his brains out."

"Jesus," Sam Sloan said.

"He said he'd do that to every one of my men, right before my eyes, unless I talked. That bastard. That fucking *bastard!*" His scream jolted the walls of the cell.

"And when they pulled the trigger, Shiloh—he was looking right at me with his one good eye. He looked at me and I was his leader and then he was dead with his brains all over and there was nothing I could do." He beat a fist on the raw cement. "Nothing I could *do*."

CHAPTER
NINETEEN ─────────────

Hermana Luz knelt by the bed in her simple white gown, hands clasped to her chest in prayer. It was hard to concentrate. These were surroundings appropriate to a rich woman, not a *poblana*, a simple country girl like her.

But it had all changed so much since the days she had walked barefoot through the provinces, speaking her Brown Mother's message of love for all Mexicans.

Then all was clear as a mountain spring. The country was ruled by men who had turned their faces from God, who were leading their people to perdition. And she had had a Vision, and set forth to lead the nation back to righteousness.

Now . . . she should be exalted. What country girl wouldn't thrill to be sleeping in a huge soft bed beneath a canopy of fine French silk? Even one who had forsworn the pleasures of world and flesh might sneak a little joy from such luxury.

And on the morning after next she would achieve that which she had dreamed so long. She would be made part of the provisional government of Mexico. And Manuel and his adviser, the strange foreigner who called himself Ian Victor and

claimed to be British—though the Virgin had told her otherwise—assured her that was temporary. Those who believed
themselves the strong men of the government were doing it to
appease the masses who sang her name and hung it on banners
from the rooflines of Mexico. But soon, her counselors told
her, soon *she* would be sole ruler of Mexico, *virreina* for the
Queen of Heaven.

But the Virgin seemed more remote now than at any time
since she had received the call. *Hermana Luz* knew her destiny
wasn't her own; she had surrendered it joyfully. But now she
felt it was no longer the Virgin who controlled that destiny.

The door opened. She spun around, ready to flare into anger:
How dare you interrrupt my devotions? But it was Manuel
Tejada with his collar open and his hair awry.

She turned back to the bed. "Do you rejoice, Little Sister?"
Manuel asked in a husky whisper. "Does your heart sing in
anticipation of your triumph?"

"I thank the Virgin for Her favor. I was doing so when you
entered."

Ignoring the hint of frost in her voice he came and sat heavily
on the edge of the bed. "Have you heard the news? The *norteamericanos* fear you, dear girl. They sent a squad of bandits
called the Guardians down here. Do you know why?"

He took her pointed chin in his fingers and turned her face
to his. Her reflex scowl melted into a look of apprehension.
He's drunk!

"They came down to kill you. You. My little *nopal*. They
came to extinguish the light of Mexico."

A strange thrill ran through her. It wasn't fear, not anything
like fear—for what did she have to fear from Death, the grinning
skeleton in *rico's* finery or peasant's sombrero and shawl she
had seen leering at her in a million Mexican paintings? All he
could do was deliver her to the bosom of the Virgin.

But yes, I am afraid, she realized with a shock. *but it isn't
the gringos I fear. And it isn't death, but the loss of my soul.*

Tejada stroked her long unbound hair with the back of a
hairy hand. The blocky gold wedding ring, encrusted with tiny
diamonds, tugged stinging at her hair.

"Soon," he whispered, breath hot on her ear. "Soon, my

little cactus flower. In two days you shall rule Mexico. And then—"

"Leave me," she said haughtily.

He stopped. His face looked like an angry pudding. Then it rearranged itself into a smile. "Yes," he said. "I do as you ask, *Hermana*." He stood and lumbered out the door.

She crawled into bed. Her skin tingled as though from an electric current. She closed her eyes, but her mind found no rest.

Then away in a corner of her mind a small white light appeared. She moistened her lips and opened her soul, and it enfolded her in radiant joy.

"Company, my friends," said Colonel Bustamante, sauntering through the open door.

Five Security Directorate thugs in fatigues lined one wall, Uzis in gloved hands. "You that afraid of us, Colonel?" McKay asked.

Bustamante laughed around the cigarette he was lighting. "I do admire your bravado in continuing to bait me, even though you now know what we can do to you if you displease us. I expected no less of you, of course.

"But as to fearing you—" He whipped the match out with a contemptuous flick of the wrist. "Rather, I respect your desperation, as one remains wary of a cornered rat.''

McKay started to open his mouth—and then it fell open all the way.

Powell Gooding stepped into the little stinking cell. He was wearing a gray suit and tie and smoking a pipe, undoubtedly to protect his delicate nostrils.

"Good afternoon, Powell," Sam Sloan said cheerfully. "Or is it evening?"

"It's evening. Gentlemen, I won't waste any time on a lengthy preamble, or—"

"Then don't," Sloan said, with a touch of icy Command Voice. "Get to the point."

Powell flushed, then nodded almost spastically. "Very well. I regret it had to come to this."

"Not like you will if we get out of this," said Toliver, who was lying on his side propped on an elbow as if he were home on the sofa watching the Super Bowl.

Gooding smiled bitterly. "Ah, the American myth surfaces again. Every man Duke Wayne or Rambo. It isn't over till it's over." He shook his head. "But is *is* over, for you. The damage that kind of retrogressive individualism has wreaked is incalculable. Look at yourselves—"

"Stuff your sociology where the sun ain't likely to shine," McKay said. "It was you who sold us out, wasn't it?"

Bill Warner had been sitting absolutely immobile, eyes fixed on Bustamante as if held in place by guy wires. Now he turned an ashen face first to McKay, then to the diplomat.

"I served the higher interests of my country—of humanity, I daresay. I—I have to thank you. Your cold-blooded murder of that traffic patrolwoman, and the callous way you boasted of it afterward, helped me to find the courage to overcome the natural bonds of comradeship forged between us by shared danger."

"Comradeship?" McKay spat out the word like shit. "You were never our comrade. You were chickenshit."

Powell blinked. "Of course you'd say that now. Of course you would. I can't let—"

"Yo, Judas my man," Tandy interrupted. "What happens to us now?"

"I—that's out of my hands. You are in the custody of the rightful authorities."

Bustamante smiled a slow thin smile. "We have friends across the water who are very interested in interviewing you gentlemen. Then again, we might feel compelled to turn you over to the followers of *Hermana Luz,* whom you came to murder." He shrugged. "We have many options, you see."

Sam Sloan smiled at the diplomat. "Get out of here before I forget those Uzis and wring your chicken neck."

Powell swallowed. He seemed about to say something. Then he changed his mind, pivoted, and walked out.

"Smart dude," Tandy said.

" 'For what is a man profited, if he shall gain the whole world, and lose his own soul?' " Bustamante quoted, looking after the diplomat. "Do you know, we didn't have to give him anything at all."

He spat on the floor and started to follow.

"Bustamante," Warner croaked. The word came out of him like a length of intestine: *"Why?"*

Bustamante made a mouth. "Just to see you crawl, *gringo*."

Alert, Sloan kicked the corporal's legs out from under him as he lunged for the secret policeman. Tandy and Toliver jumped on their leader, pinning him frothing and shrieking to the cement.

The uniforms looked pleased to hustle out after their leader in spite of their guns.

Bustamante's laugh echoed through the door as he walked off down the hall.

Sam Sloan was wakened from a surprisingly sound sleep by a boot to the ribs. He rolled over to see a uniformed FSD man leaning over him. The policeman yelled something in Spanish, spraying him with garlic-flavored spittle.

"I get the message," Sloan said, working his way to his feet. He didn't feel much better than McKay looked.

He and McKay traded glances. They knew each other well enough to trade thoughts as well: *Wait for a chance, then go for it.* But there were no chances. Their arms were immoblized by nylon wraps quickly and efficiently under the guns of the guards.

In the corridor they found Tom, Casey, Shig, and Richard, similarly cuffed and guarded. Casey had a black eye and Tom had been battered on some, but it looked as if McKay had been worked over the worst of all.

"You guys all right?" McKay asked.

"Well as could be expected, Billy."

Under the eye of a stocky officer the guards prodded them down corridors, into a paved courtyard, and into the back of a dark van with the familiar mesh windows.

It was an oak-paneled office. The walls were decked with soccer memorabilia, pictures of saints, and what Sam Sloan would've sworn was a picture of a prize bull, not a fighter but a Charolais.

He glanced left to McKay and Rogers and right to Casey. *At least we have chairs.*

The fat man with the sweat stains in the armpits of his

uniform shifted his weight, unwrapped a caramel from a silver
bowl on his desk, and popped it in his mouth. The room smelled
faintly of farts.

He chewed for a moment, periodically running his tongue
over his lips. Then he spoke in Spanish while a diminutive
middle-aged aide translated.

"Gentlemen, I cannot tell you how much pleasure it gives
me to see you. Cipriano Fuentes at your service. I have the
honor of being chief of police for Mexico City."

"Cut the crap," McKay said, lolling his head back on his
neck and glaring at the cop from a blackened eye. "We ain't
gonna tell you nothin'."

The aide looked as if he was about to swallow his tongue.
His eyes whipsawed back and forth between the captives and
the chief of police several times before he spoke. From Casey's
stifled giggle Sam gathered McKay's speech was being cen-
sored.

"But I know all about you already. You have come to do
away with *Hermana Luz*.

"That's why I freed you from the clutches of that ogre
Morales. So you can finish what you came to do."

CHAPTER
TWENTY

As the open jeep rolled slowly along the blank face of the wall, the sergeant yawned.

"Too late to be out and about, at least if you're sober, huh?" said Ignacio the driver, with a gaptoothed grin.

The sergeant scowled. That was his thought exactly, but it would be bad for discipline to say so. And discipline was all-important now, if the army was at last to wrest power from the shiftless, greedy civilians who had mismanaged the country's affairs for so long.

"Why the hell do we got to guard this bitch, anyway?" asked Juan, draped lazily on the wooden stock of his pintle-mounted machinegun. "A week ago we was supposed to be guarding the city from her. Now we're guarding her from the city. Don't make no sense."

"It doesn't have to," the sergeant said loftily. "You are paid to be a soldier, not to understand."

Juan gave the horns to the fat back of the sergeant's neck. His A-gunner stifled a giggle.

The sergeant was feeling even more superior than usual. The

NCO's network knew everything that went on, of course. They knew all the details of General Barela's cunning plan to neutralize not only the *Cristeros* but the evil man they called the Spider. The private soldiers, of course, were ignorant of the scheme, as they were of most things.

"We should knock this off and go find a whorehouse," said Beto, the assistant gunner.

"*Hermana Luz* has to get her beauty sleep," the driver said. "She's got a big day tomorrow."

"Wouldn't you just love to pull duty for the ceremony?" Beto said with a leer. "Those señoritas start to get the Spirit in 'em, their skirts just sort of float up above their pretty little heads."

The sergeant sniffed. Then again, *Hermana Luz* was a heretic, so perhaps his remarks, while coarse, weren't really blasphemy. You had to keep a close eye on the ranks, though. No telling what they'd get up to. They were like the country at large: in constant need of firm discipline.

The jeep rounded the corner onto a narrow side street lined with trees and three-story colonial buildings. A figure lay slumped in the street with one arm beneath him and the other outflung. A mostly empty tequila bottle lay a few centimeters from his fingers.

The sergeant motioned for the driver to stop with a white gloved hand. "Get him out of the way," he ordered the A-gunner.

Beto jumped out and bebopped over to the drunk. He gave him a combat boot in the ribs. "All right, *cuate,* pick it up and get it out of here. *Hermana Luz* don't want no fuckin' *borrachos* snoring outside her window."

With surprising alacrity for a drunk the man rolled over. He had a monkey face, an evil grin, and a big pistol with an even bigger silencer screwed onto the end of it. Beto opened his mouth to scream.

The bullet chipped his front two teeth and blasted out the back of his head.

Two more muffled thumps came from behind a car parked right next to the jeep. Juan coughed and subsided into the rear seat. The sergant felt the jeep rock and turned to see an arm wrapped around the driver's neck. The uniform was Mexican

Army tan, but the forearm and the hand that drove a gleaming knife into the side of Ignacio's throat were black as the night.

The sergeant grabbed for his own chrome-plated sidearm. A weight thumped in the jeep right behind him. Something flicked before his eyes, and then there was intolerable constriction shutting off his windpipe, and a sudden agony in his throat, and he saw his blood gush in black wave across the dashboard, and he hoped most fervently that *Hermana Luz* wasn't truly the emissary of the Virgin.

Tandy and Buck, all but bursting out of their Mexican Army uniforms, dragged the bodies into the shadows. Richard Gallegos jumped to his feet, stripping off his floppy shirt and trousers to reveal an immaculate lieutenant's uniform beneath. Fastidious as always, Shig left his garrote embedded in the fat sergeant's neck as his huskier teammates hauled him off.

He climbed into the driver's seat. He was pure *sansei,* third-generation Japanese-American, but both Raúl and Chief Fuentes had assured him he could pass for a Mexican as long as he didn't open his mouth. Any talking would be handled by Gallegos, whose border accent would pass muster as *norteño.*

The bodies stuffed in the trunk of a car—thoughtfully provided from the impound lot, courtesy of the Mexico City police department—Tandy and Buck crammed their old-style GI surplus pot helmets well down on their heads. Toliver climbed dubiously into the back of the jeep next to the machinegun. With his own helmet pulled low, Warner was dark enough not to arouse much suspicion; big, fair Toliver couldn't stand any examination at all.

But Warner wanted to be on the ground with Tandy and Raúl, who wore corporal's insignia and would handle any conversation. And Warner was the honcho.

Still, it was unlikely Toliver would be spotted, if he slouched. There weren't many casual passersby, since the FSD goons, the *Cristeros,* and the army had all been discouraging curiosity since *Hermana Luz* had taken up residence. And nobody who was abroad at this hour of the morning was going to wonder why there were three men in the jeep rather than four—this was the Mexican Army. Only a duty officer might be curious. That was why Toliver had the silenced .45 Richard had borrowed from the Guardians resting next to his M-203 on the floor by his feet.

Warner held a second silenced Guardian .45 negligently in one fist. He was carryong O'Neal's M-203 slung and wore a canvas vest with a dozen 40-mm rounds carried in reinforced pockets. Willy Peter hand grenades hung from rings sewn down both sides of the vest.

He nodded. "551st ready," he whispered. The microphone taped to his larynx picked up the words as easily as if he'd spoken them aloud and piped them through his borrowed communicator. His blue eyes glared with quiet fury from the shadow of his helmet as he melted back into the darkness gathered by the wall.

Buck Toliver signaled Shig to put the jeep in gear. As they drove away he thumbed the suppress button on the communicator in his own pocket. "So where the hell are the *other* five hundred and fifty Special Duty Squads now that we need 'em?"

In the headquarters of the Mexico City Police Department, Cipriano Fuentes smiled. The code word had just come over the radiotelephone: the *norteamericanos* were in position.

How fortuitous it was that *la Araña's* trusted aide Major Yniquez had chosen to perform an indiscretion with a boy who happened to be a cousin of one of *Fuentes's* trusted aides. Spider Morales liked to have a handle on those closest to him. It never seemed to have occurred to him others could grasp those handles, too.

Or maybe it never occurred to him that the fat, complacent, and, yes, stupid Chief Fuentes would have the wherewithal to get hold of such a handle. Well, Fuentes was willing to acknowledge that he was all those things. But he was one additional thing.

He was fighting for his life.

He wrested the handset from where it was trapped between shoulder and jowl, lowered his hand to punch a finger at the bottom on his telephone. A voice answered before he heard the ring from the exchange.

"*Fiat lux,*" he said, and farted happily.

"*¿Qué?*"

"Let there be light, you idiot."

"Oh. *Sí*, Señor Jefe."

Dressed in black, faces painted black, black stocking caps on their heads, the Guardians emerged from the doorway of the apartment whose roof McKay, Rogers, and Warner had watched the villa from a century ago or night before last, depending on whether you went by subjective time or what the clocks said. McKay slammed face first against the wall. Tom Rogers swarmed up his back like a monkey, carrying a coil of blackened nylon rope over his shoulder. He slapped a Kevlar mat over top of the broken glass that topped the wall and climbed up.

He did a quick check of the grounds. No *Cristeros* were in sight. He turned, covering with his silenced MP-5, while Casey came dashing across the narrow street and up onto McKay's shoulders. The former fighter jock bellied over the mat, dropped to the ground inside, unslinging his MAC-10, keen eyes searching the shadows between them and the big white house.

An instant later Sam dropped next to him, holding one end of the rope. Sloan and Rogers dogged it while McKay climbed it. When he was inside, Tom leapt to the ground with the mat and the rope. He stuck them under a bush.

"We're in," McKay subvocalized. It was Warner's cue to bring Tandy and Raúl in across the far wall to provide support on the ground. Toliver's jeep was put on alert to come play Rat Patrol to the rescue if necessary.

Silent as panthers, the Guardians moved toward the villa that gleamed faintly in the starlight.

"*Hijo de la chingada*," the sergeant from the Department for the Prevention of Delinquency—a wholly owned subsidiary of the Mexico City police—climbed out of the unmarked Brazilian station wagon and slammed the door. The plainclothesman behind the wheel sank down, trying to make himself invisible as his superior stamped toward the National Palace, still carrying the electronic hand detonator in one hand.

The lights were on in the palace. Mexico's elected representatives were debating whether to attend the ceremony for *Hermana Luz* in the morning, as if anyone gave a good God damn.

The DPD sergeant didn't. What he gave a damn about was he'd tried the detonator five times without effect.

He was letting himself into a side service entrance when the backup warning beeper of a forklift over doing last-minute work on the dais in the Zócalo set off the radio controlled fuses affixed to a dozen fifty-liter disinfectant drums filled with gasoline in the basement about eight meters from where he stood.

The Guardians had the diversion *Jefe* Fuentes had promised them.

Hermana Luz sat in a satin-cushioned chair, watching in a mirror as a pair of Indian maids combed out her long black hair. *Is this really me?* she wondered. *Do I belong here?*

She knew the answer to the second question, at least.

"Now, Little Sister," a stout maid chided, "don't fidget! You want to look your best tomorrow, don't you?"

"It hardly matters, Eufémia," she said dreamily.

"Tut! Don't talk like that, child. Of course it matters. You want to make the Virgin proud, don't you? Now, when I was a mere slip of a girl like you—''

The glass of the window shattered, collapsing inwards in a glittering, sliding, crashing torrent.

Herman Luz's eyes flicked upward into the mirror. A man dressed all in black was lunging into the room even as the glass fell to the wood parquetry floor. He seemed to be moving in slow motion, the way they did sometimes on the television in the village where she was raised. She heard each beat of her heart in her ears, distinct and spaced what seemed many seconds apart.

"*¡Mira, el Cuco!*" screamed Eufémia, the comb falling from her hand: *Look, the bogeyman!*

Her cry snapped the spell. Time flowed normally. *Hermana Luz* leapt to her feet and turned in a whirl of white silk nightgown. A second, taller intruder was stepping between the billowing curtains.

Her other maid, screaming like a cat in heat, was chugging for the door as fast as her plump legs could carry her. The first man fired the strange, stubby weapon he held in his hands. It made a funny sound, a hard rapping, not like a real gun at all. But the splinters that flew from the top of the doorframe were an unmistakable message. The maid gave a last despairing yip and collapsed to the floor.

"Get down on the floor," the man who had shot ordered in clear but curiously accented Spanish.

But Eufémia put her bulk between *Hermana Luz* and the intruders, spreading her arms protectively. "You won't harm Sister Light while I live, you atheists," she declared.

Casey Wilson looked at Tom Rogers. Rogers looked back. Casey felt a surge of relief. He'd been afraid Tom would just gun the girl down. That was their mission, of course, what they'd crawled through Hell to accomplish. But now that they were here looking the girl in the eye it didn't seem like such a great idea.

For one thing, the girl was awfully pretty. Her unplucked eyebrows only added to the effect, somehow. So slender and fine-boned, yet projecting a feel of strength as she faced them without a sign of fear.

"Secure the door, Case," Tom said. Casey swiped at a strand of hair that was trying to escape from his cap and started forward.

The girl lunged for him.

Only fighter-pilot reflexes stopped him from ripping her apart with a burst from his MAC-10. Then her arms were around his neck and she was crying, "You're the one, the one from my vision! The one who's come to rescue me!"

CHAPTER
TWENTY-ONE ─────

McKay and Sloan crouched at the base of the wall, trying to cover in all directions at once. Their eyes kept getting drawn back to the clouds of yellow flame boiling up from the National Palace. The sirens were a real demon's chorus in that direction. Chief Fuentes had definitely come across with the promised diversion.

That don't mean I trust him any farther than I can throw him, he thought.

Fortunately the fire wasn't bright enough to impair their night vision. They had good bushes to hide in. They hadn't seen any sign of *Cristeros* patrolling among the jacaranda and mimosa trees of the grounds. They were there; the Guardians had skirted a couple of groups on their way to the big house. But they were getting complacent, content to find a place to park their butts and while their watch away.

"Our luck is definitely in," Sam Sloan subvocalized. He was tense as a whippet beside McKay; McKay had never seen the former naval officer so keyed.

"You never want to say shit like that," he said. It was true: Tom and Case were agile as acrobats. But you didn't say it; it

was like mentioning when somebody was pitching a perfect game. Had anybody wandered past as they were climbing over each other from ground to balcony and from second floor balcony to third floor they would have been reenacting the Fall of the Flying Wallendas right here.

They both winced as one to the crash of breaking glass from above. They heard feminine screams, then a quick stutter of silenced gunfire.

Sam swallowed visibly and looked at McKay. His eyes were huge as an old-fashioned minstrel-show actor's in his blacked-out face.

"Nobody heard," he subvocalized. *"Just sounds loud 'cause we're expecting it."* But he knew that wasn't Sam's problem.

Well, fuck a bunch of this Sister Light, he thought savagely. *She's killed enough people. It's come down payback time.*

"McKay." It was Toliver's rasp, sounding alien in his bone phone. *"Car coming through the gates."*

"Roger." No biggie; Sister Light's room was at the rear of the mansion, just where the useful Major Yniquez said it'd be. But it was good to know company was on the way, for safety's sake.

From above came more shots, no noisier than a cap gun but still horribly loud in taut-stretched eardrums. He felt Sloan flinch. *That's it,* he thought.

Casey Wilson stood flatfooted while this strange girl clung to him with strong brown hands. He was a Guardian, he'd been the hottest pilot since Yeager, he'd been something of a ladies' man. But nothing in his experience gave him much clue as to how to handle *this.*

He looked to Rogers. His heart was in his throat. He'd killed before—he'd lost count of how many he'd killed, at least if you spoke of people and not airplanes. He was sure he'd killed kids, teenage girls not so different from this one, with his bombs in the Mideast.

But to kill a beautiful girl clinging to him like a lost lover— that was a new dimension. One he had no desire to explore.

"Take me with you," she said in soft Spanish. "Please. I must get away from this place."

And Tom Rogers, that hard, cold man—shrugged.

Had he given the sign, Casey would have killed her. He was a Guardian, and his duty right now was to bow to the older man's judgment, that had kept them alive so many times. Instead—and he *knew* this, as if Rogers had spoken aloud—his partner was saying, it's our job to take her out, and if she comes with us, the *Cristeros* will be as leaderless as if we killed her. So why not?

Besides, Casey thought, *we can always finish the job later*. He swallowed hard.

"All right," he said in Spanish. "You can come with us."

She kissed him on the lips.

The door opened. "*Hermana Luz,* is something the matter?" asked a man in *campesino* garb with a rifle slung over his shoulder. His eyes got very wide.

Tom shot him past Casey's right biceps. "*Let's get out of here,*" he hissed.

Hunkered down in shrubs forty meters from the front drive, Warner, Tandy, and Raúl watched a long gray Mercedes limo slide between the spike-tipped wrought-iron gates and go crunching along the gravel toward the mansion.

Warner stiffened. He squinted, staring hard at the car. "Mother *fucker,*" he whispered.

"*What's that? Warner?*" McKay's voice rapped in his ear. "*Is something happening?*"

Ignoring him, Warner stood up and began to run full out after the limo.

"What the fuck is that idiot up to?" McKay demanded in an angry whisper. He didn't like what he'd heard in the Texican leader's voice.

"*Coming down,*" Tom radioed. The black rope slithered down into the bush behind McKay.

McKay was straining every sense, expecting at any instant to hear hell break loose nearby. Instead cloth fell across his vision like curtains, and a heavy weight came down on his shoulders.

"Jesus *Christ!*" Only survival reflexes burned-in on a hundred battlefields made the exclamation come out a whisper instead of a full-voiced bellow. Still keeping his MP-5 as ready as possible with one hand he clapped the other to his shoulder.

It came in contact with smooth, bare flesh. Nights of Braille between the sheets told him almost at once that he had a pair of young strong, female legs around his neck. A rasp on the stubble at the back of his neck told him the young, strong female in question wasn't wearing underwear.

"Oh, wow, Billy, I'm sorry," Casey said, dropping lightly beside his leader. "I guess I swung her out too far before I let her down."

If rank had meant anything among the Guardians, McKay would've busted them all back to E-1 on the spot. Casey, Sam, Tom—shit, he'd bust himself for getting his ass into this situation. "Will somebody kindly tell me *what the fuck is going on?*"

The girl was removed from his neck. When the last of the silk slipped off his face and he got a look at her standing with her arms around Casey he had a twinge of regret she hadn't come down in front of him instead. She definitely fit his requirements for a midnight snack.

"Oh, sweet Virgin!" a voice screeched from the window above. "They're kidnapping Sister Light!"

Casey made a face and grabbed the girl's arm. "Later, Billy." He sprayed the window with a burst from his Ingram and lit out into the night.

The Mercedes rolled to a stop on the half-moon drive before the mansion's portico. Federal Security Directorate flunkies in business suits popped out to usher forth their boss

One heard the crackling of someone running on gravel and turned to see a bareheaded soldier running towards them. He frowned. The army was allied with the FSD for the moment, but only a fool trusted the army; it would be just like those ribbon-decked pigs to foul up the Directorate's strategy by betraying them first. His hand went for the Skorpion in his shoulder holster.

At a range of under ten feet the 40-mm Multiple Projectile round from the launcher slung under Bill Warner's rifle simply tore his head off.

A second secret policeman stood with his hand on the handle of the half-opened door. Warner buttstroked him out of the way, busting the plastic stock of the M-16. He slapped the barrel onto the top of the car and shot a third who came up on the driver's side with a gun in his hand.

Inside, Colonel Bustamante worked his own Skorpion out of its shoulder holster, pressed the muzzle to the inside of the door, and fired full-automatic. The sharp 7.65-mm bullets punched right through the sheet metal and lanced into Warner's leg.

Crouching just past the border of the light that fell from the great house's entrance, Raúl and Tandy watched in horror as Warner sagged away from the limo.

"We must help him," Raúl said, starting forward.

Tandy stopped him with a hand on his arm. "*No*. No, dammit, we can't. We gotta cover the others."

Raúl glanced back and saw the tear running down the man's black cheek. He stayed where he was.

Warner dropped his rifle and yanked open the door. Bustamante had been pushing against it with his pistol, fighting the recoil. He half-fell from the car. Warner grabbed his wrist and shoved his arm back hard against the doorframe.

Bustamante howled like a wolf as his elbow snapped.

Quick as a terrier taking a rat Warner had the colonel out of the car with his suit coat yanked halfway down his back, pinning good arm and useless one alike. He spun him around, putting Bustamante between him and the nervously circling Security Directorate cops.

He peeled a big WP grenade from his vest, pulled the pin with his teeth, just like in all the John Wayne movies, and stuffed the can of molten death down the front of Bustamante's white shirt. The colonel's eyes practically exploded in horror.

"You'll never get away with this," Bustamante shrieked.

Warner grinned down into his face. "Who said I wanted to get away?" Still holding the colonel's jacket with one hand he reached up and tore loose a handful of grenade pins.

"Payback's a mother," he said. The first grenade blew.

Then all the rest.

Halfway to the wall half a dozen *Cristeros* stumbled in front of the Guardians. Casey sprayed them wildly with his Ingram, which was about the only way you could fire the damned thing, even if you used both hands.

A couple went down. Sloan and Rogers chopped the others, except for one who appeared right in McKay's path. The former marine caught him with a straight right in the face that snapped his neck.

Behind them they heard a flurry of shots. Bullets clipped twigs over their heads, but McKay had the impression much of the shooting was on the far side of the house.

At the wall they paused to catch their breath while Rogers grabbed his rope and mat. *"Warner, Toliver,"* McKay called, slinging his MP-5, and making a step of his hands for Rogers. *"We're set to pull out."*

"On our way," Toliver acknowledged as Rogers went back up the wall.

"Where the fuck is Warner?"

"No idea, McKay."

McKay unslung his MP-5. Casey's girlfriend was still hanging on as if she'd been grafted to his arm. "Jesus, Casey, leave it to you to pick up a bimbo in the middle of a firefight."

"I wonder why nobody's chasing us?" Casey asked the air.

From the other side of the house a fireworks display erupted. There were screams, and starfish arms of Willy Peter streaking in all directions, and a booming like an artillery barrage.

"Great Caesar's ghost!" Sloan exclaimed. "What's *that?*"

Rogers frowned from the top of the wall. What he was still doing up there was a mystery to McKay; maybe he had liquid helium in his veins. It had taken all McKay's self-control to keep from making love to the exquisitely manicured turf.

"Forty mike-mikes," he said. "We'd better hurry."

" 'Great Caesar's ghost'?" McKay said to Sloan. "You actually *said* that?"

Sloan looked sheepish. "I read too many Superman comics as a kid. What can I tell you."

Toliver's jeep was waiting when they tumbled over the wall. The Texican was hanging off the MAG, eyes scanning the walls and street.

"Where'd you get the piece?" he asked as McKay helped the girl into the car with a hand on the fanny.

"Ask Case. He found her. Let's go find that dumb fuck

Warner." Gallegos grinned at McKay and burned rubber.

As they reached the gate two unmistakable stun grenades flashed off right inside it. "*Okay,*" Toliver said. He chopped three guards with precise bursts from his machinegun.

Tandy and Raúl hit the gate, nailing a last dazzled *Cristero* sentry on the run. "Where's Warner?" McKay asked as they piled any which way onto the overladen jeep.

"Back there." Tandy jerked his head toward the mansion. They could see the light of a bodacious bonfire dancing on its upper stories from here. "He saw that fucker Bustamante."

The Guardians stared at the villa. The Mercedes' gas tank finally cooked off with a *whoom!*, sending a mushroom cloud of yellow-orange fire up into the hazy sky.

"*Ave atque vale,*" Sam said softly.

"Gesundheit," McKay said. "Richard, get us out of here."

People were running up the drive at them. Toliver gave them a burst as Gallegos peeled out.

Cristeros were spilling out of the buildings facing the compound's walls, clutching assorted firearms. The Guardians and the 551st survivors sent them flying in all directions with a hail of gunfire.

"You don't have to answer this if you don't want to, Casey," McKay said, dropping a spent magazine and clicking another into his submachine gun's well as Gallegos took a corner on two wheels. A few *Cristeros* followed them. Tandy and Raúl discouraged them with their M-16s. "But just who is this woman we have with us?"

"Oh. Her." He glanced at Rogers. "She's, uh, *Hermana Luz,* Billy. She wanted to come with us."

McKay turned around and stared. The girl brushed a strand of hair from her eyes and smiled shyly.

"Casey, do me one favor," he said.

"Anything, Billy."

"If I ever ask you to explain this to me, just shoot me. Okay?"

"Where are we bugging out to, McKay?" Richard asked, hunched down behind the wheel and in general getting off on playing Unser Brothers.

"Well, the safe house Fuentes arranged for us—" Sloan began.

"Fuck the safe house," McKay said. "We're not sticking in

town. Especially not with her in our back pocket."

"But Fuentes had it all worked out for us," Shigeo protested. "He could get angry if we change the plan."

"How do we know what his plan really is? He blew up the National Palace, for Christ's sake. He may be a perfectly nice man for somebody who farts that much, but right now we could be mighty embarrassing to him. And he don't look like a man who resists temptation all that God-damned fiercely. I think it's best if we blow this burg, all right?"

"But where will we go?" Sloan asked. "They'll be watching the airport."

"And is almost dawn, and this is Mexico City," Raúl said. "We no can drive out. Traffic, she jams."

"Hey, it's cool. Richard, remember that little detour we took, before our slumber party with Bustamante?"

Gallegos turned a bloodless face to him. "You're not thinking—"

"Oh, yes I am."

"You're nuts, McKay."

"I'm here, ain't I? Now, FIDO: Fuck It and Drive On."

CHAPTER
TWENTY-TWO ─────

The crew in the emplacement atop the old diesel engine were just finishing their last Thermos of coffee by the light of dawn, in order to be awake when their relief showed up, when a little metal can with a rounded snout dropped in amongst them and began to spit white smoke. The startled soldiers' eyes began to water furiously.

They were quick on the uptake. Their watch had ended prematurely. Three managed to get to the steel rungs welded in ladders down either side of the engine. Two others just sort of swan-dived off the top. One busted both legs on the cement. The other was already gimping off when two of his companions passed him.

The last man of the watch stood around blinking. One of the party of unauthorized but heavily armed personnel in the jeep bouncing over the rails into the depths of Mexico City's central railyard shot him with an M-16.

"You're sure you can run this thing?" McKay asked dubiously as everybody spilled out and started tossing gear through the open door of the sleeper car behind the engine.

Casey and Richard Gallegos both gave him thumbs-up. "Piece of cake," Casey said.

"Right."

The two clambered into the engine with *Hermana Luz* right behind them. McKay shook his head and ran back with Tom to try to figure out how to decouple the rest of the train aft of the one car.

They'd just got it figured out when two mighty blasts of an airhorn practically lifted them out of their socks.

"Jesus, *Christ*, Casey!" McKay hollered, ostensibly over the communicator, though his bellow wasn't much quieter than the horn. "Will you grow up? What the hell are you doing?"

"Gee, Billy, I'm sorry. But we've got company. I, like, thought you'd want to know."

McKay and Rogers looked up. There was this gigantic mob streaming toward them across the railyards. It reminded McKay of that movie about the army ants they always used to show on late-night TV, the one with Joan Collins in it before her last four or five facelifts.

"Son of a bitch," McKay said. He started slogging through the cinders toward the engine. "Tom, get inside. One of you Texican troopies come play A-gunner for me, pronto."

He went up the rungs as if he had a rocket in his ass. The emplacement up top consisted of a spiderweb arrangement of metal struts with sandbags piled onto it. At close range it looked like nothing so much as the makeshift strongpoint stuck on Mad Max's semi in *The Road Warrior*. It wasn't a happy thought, considering how that worked out.

On the other hand, if the good guys'd had a good ol' Browning M-2 in that movie, Wez, the Humongous, and all their merry mohawked friends would've eaten shit and died Big Time. He settled in behind the gun and opened the feed tray.

Shigeo came crawling up over the top with a heavy box of ammo on his shoulder. "This was down below," he grunted, dropping it into the nest and crawling in after it. "Thought it might come in handy."

"Might," McKay agreed, eyeing the horde. It was getting closer. He opened the box already in the nest, was relieved to find ammo in it, and dropped the end of a belt into the receiver.

The size and heft of the linked cartridges reassured him.

"Does anyone have any idea who these people are? They wouldn't maybe be the Jaycees come to wave as we bid farewell to their lovely city?"

"They're singing," Sloan said.

"Isn't that nice? And who do we know who sings, boys and girl?" Fatigue and the aftermath of an adrenaline hellride was making him lightheaded. *Get a hold of yourself,* he thought sternly.

"*Hermana Luz* says it's her people," Casey reported. "They don't want to let her leave."

By now McKay had recognized the song. It was the one that went, basically, I'm a Mexican, I'm a Christian, tra la, tra la, kill 'em all and let God sort 'em out, tra la.

"Time for another atrocity," he commented, and squeezed the butterfly triggers. The gun seemed to shake the whole engine as it belched a slow, short burst.

Just those few rounds knocked a big hole out of the mob. The heavy slugs would go through most buildings. They could go through ten or twenty people or even more, if they all obligingly lined up. The problem was, these were fanatics. *Plentiful* fanatics.

"Casey, do you think this train might be leaving anytime soon?"

"Trains never run on time in this country, McKay."

"Fuck you, Toliver." Small arms fire began to pop from the crowd. McKay heard bullets crack over his head as rifles in the sleeper car responded. "Casey, the peasants with torches are getting close and Frankenstein really wants to go bye-bye."

The response was an airhorn blast that lifted him right off the roof. The engine vibrated and slowly began to chug into motion. "Casey, knock it off with that goddam horn! Give me a break, will you?"

"We have to blow the horn," Gallegos said, obviously leaning over to talk into Casey's throat mike. "Regulations."

"Everyone's comedian."

The abbreviated train gathered speed much quicker than it appeared to, and was pulling well out ahead of the mob before it reached the track. McKay sighed heavily and swung the

MG's barrel skyward. "So much for you."

"More out front, Billy," Casey reported.

McKay craned his neck. Sure enough, the tracks ahead were black with people, shouting, singing, waving banners.

"Put the hammer down, Casey," he ordered. He grimaced at Shig. "This is gonna be gross."

Casey was finally getting the feel of a train. It didn't handle very much like an F-16. It was simpler, for one thing. You only had to deal with two dimensions. In fact, you pretty much only had to cope with *one* dimension. He felt it come alive in his hands, moving fast and ever faster.

He put an arm around *Hermana Luz's* slim shoulders. "Better close your eyes, kid," he warned.

Maybe he was as much a monster as Gooding claimed—and it was a pisser that they couldn't cancel that fucker's credit cards for him before blowing town—but McKay had to watch. A few doubting souls broke and ran as the train hurtled down on them. The rest held firm, singing about the Virgin and raising adoring arms as if to pluck their prophetess out of the train.

They splashed.

A scream of a hundred voices dwarfed the air horn. For a horrible moment McKay imagined the train was skating, losing traction on a slick of blood and flesh and human grease. Blood drenched the sides of the sleeper like graffiti on a New York subway car.

Soaked head to toe in blood like ancient Aztec priests, *Cristeros* ran after the train, shouting and throwing stones. *Hermana Luz* wept. She wasn't alone.

Fast as the train was moving, it seemed to take forever to leave the running fanatics behind. It took longer to outpace the cries of the injured, the legless, and the crushed.

But at last the *Cristeros* fell behind. The train clattered north through affluent suburbs and squatters' camps. McKay let himself slide lower and lower in the nest while the sun, still only just above the rocky rim of the Valley of Mexico, seemed to weight down his eyelids as if its light was lead.

Shig settled himself comfortably across from him. He adjusted his glasses and smiled.

"Since we're here, let me tell you something about the fascinating and marvelous world of trains," he said.

"They could stop us anytime," McKay said, sipping instant coffee made with water heated on a camp stove that had somehow survived the wars. "Just block the tracks. Even switch us onto a siding somewhere."

"We've been slowing to check out every switchpoint, or whatever you call them," Casey said. Like McKay he was taking a break in the sleeper. Sister Light sat beside him with her amber eyes aglow. "They've all been open."

"They won't think of it," Toliver predicted.

"He has right," Raúl said. "That would no be the *macho* way, no?"

News from Mexico City filtered in all day. Some soldier had left a Sony ghetto blaster aboard. Whenever it began to fade the Guardians could always use their satellite uplink/downlink and radio set to follow the news, or get updates from Texas, California—or Washington, which was going crazy.

It seemed that the army had treacherously attacked the villa in which *Hermana Luz* was living. She had either been abducted or killed—speculation ran wild—though her body had not yet been found. The grieving thousands of faithful, in concert with the ever-vigilant Federal Security Directorate, had launched massive reprisal attacks on the army, forcing General Barelas to flee into exile. Manuel Tejada broke down when he was being interviewed on nationwide TV and had to be escorted off the set.

In other news, Police Chief Fuentes announced that several solid leads had been unearthed in last night's disastrous fire in the National Palace. Arson was strongly suspected. . . .

Rogers sat in the emplacement with McKay, side by side with the wind at their backs. "So, what's the real story with this *Hermana Luz* anyway?" McKay asked. He had carefully disabled his throat mike.

Rogers watched Mexico unreel behind the train for a while. "She says she had a vision of the Virgin the night before last," he said, choosing his words carefully. "The Virgin told her that she had been misled by evil men who, uh, who warped her mission to their own ends. That what was supposed to be a message of love wound up bringing death and misery to a lot of people."

"No shit. You mean, the kid claims not to *know* her precious *Cristeros* were going through north Mexico and south Texas like a plague of locusts?"

"She didn't know at the time."

"Shit."

"I think it's true. She's not, you know, very sophisticated. And this Tejada kept her real insulated, used her to build power for himself. Just like the vision said."

"He had help."

Rogers shrugged. Vesensky had been involved in this mess, no question. But he had gone by the time they reached Mexico; both men were sure of it without exactly knowing why. Maybe they could smell him.

"Anyway, this vision. The Virgin released *Hermana Luz* from her vows. I guess She told her to go off and live her own life and not worry about crusading anymore. And that we would come and rescue her from Tejada and them. Casey specifically."

"Casey *specifically?*"

Rogers shrugged again. "She acted like she knew him, Billy."

McKay eyed him. "Do you really buy this vision crap, Tommy?"

"I don't know, Billy. I'm not a Catholic." He sounded uncomfortable.

"Great. That's a big help." He stared off at the wide and tawny land until his eyes watered. "So we should maybe not put a bullet in the back of her head and dump her sometime when Case ain't looking?"

"I don't think so, Billy. She really wasn't to blame for all the bad stuff. And it'd upset Casey."

"Yeah. I guess it would."

"It's funny," Raúl remarked sometime after dark. "I was the

only one who came here looking for death. And I am still alive."

"Yeah," McKay said. "Life's a bitch and then you don't die."

Ten hours later they rolled across the border into the Republic of Texas.

EPILOGUE ────────────

The crowd quieted as Manuel Tejada spread his arms. They filled the Zócalo to overflowing, clear to the scorched facade of the National Palace.

As they'll fill the nation, before I'm done with them.

"My children," he said, his voice booming from three-story speakers, "behold that which the treacherous *gringos* have taken from you." He gestured and the enormous TV screen behind him filled with a close-up of *Hermana Luz*'s face, caught in a moment of intense piety and looking breathtakingly lovely.

His own heart felt briefly as if a spectral fist had squeezed it. *My own lost love,* he thought, *where are you now?* But he could not afford to dwell too long on what he'd lost. More important was what he had to gain, thanks to the long-distance guidance of the invaluable "Ian Victor."

Maybe the *norteamericanos* would give *Hermana Luz* back; certainly, that mewling fool Gooding kept insisting his government would do anything at all to avoid friction with its neighbor to the south. More likely she was gone forever. But then, the provinces were full of lovely peasant girls. They were there for the plucking . . . if you were president.

"Look upon the holy features of our personal messenger from the Virgin of Guadalupe, Mother to us all." The crowd was murmuring now, a sound that swelled like a gathering storm. The power was palpable, almost sexual. *I'm unstoppable,* he thought. *Unstoppable.*

"She is gone. But she remains with us in spirit. Therefore I call upon you to rise up, demand that—"

The crowd gasped.

Tejada tried to plow on, but no one was paying attention. Everyone in the vast crowd was staring . . . *past* him.

He turned.

The lovely, piquant face on the screen had come to life. The eyes blinked, the daintily turned nostrils flared delicately to the well-remembered rhythm of her breathing.

"*Dios,*" Tejada breathed. His knees went weak.

"Children of the Brown Virgin," the face said, and the crowd sighed, for the voice was Hers. "Listen to me, who was your Sister Light."

Somewhere a voice cried in despair, and the voice had many throats. "Do not despair, my people. Know that I have gone from among you voluntarily."

The crowd made an incoherent sound of disbelief and incomprehension. "I was betrayed," the face said. "The Blessed Virgin who spoke through me was betrayed, by men who perverted Her message of love to words of hate. Many evil deeds were done in my name—and worse, in Hers.

"Yet the fault lies not with those who spread destruction, for their hearts were pure. The fault belongs to those who misled them. Who put lies in my mouth. Who lied to me, who tried to manipulate me, in order to enslave us all, all Mexicans, in the interest of a foreign power—"

The crowd was growling now, a tidal surge of rage. "No, wait!" Tejada screamed. "Don't listen to her! It's lies, she's being forced—" He waved his hands as if to obscure the giant screen.

"—foremost among them is Manuel Tejada Riojos, my most trusted adviser. He knowingly manipulated me—and knowingly allowed himself to be manipulated by an agent of Chairman Maximov of the Federated States of Europe, an agent who was formerly a member of the Soviet KGB—"

They were screaming out there now, screaming in fury. *Hermana Luz* had touched them on the rawest nerve of all.

"In the name of the Queen of Heaven," the girl said in a voice to fill the world, "and of Christ our King, I call upon you to turn away from hate, to end the senseless killing and live out your lives in loving service. As I myself shall do.

"I spoke the words the Virgin inspired in me. Now by her inspiration I lay aside my mantle of prophecy. I am again what I always was: a plain *mestiza,* a proud daughter of Mexico.

"I leave you now in love." And the face once again froze into immobility.

Slowly, by inches it seemed, the crowd closed in upon Manuel Tejada. Sobbing, pleading, he fell to his knees. He crossed himself, and with a great scream of fury they broke upon him like the surf.

Sister Light's farewell address got the best ratings in the history of Mexican televison. Some said it was the first real miracle of the electronic age.

Apolinar Morales, known as *la Araña,* decided to take a protracted trip in South America for reasons of health.

So did the local TV technicians who had cooperated long-distance with a fifteen-year-old satellite communications whiz in the Freehold named Kathy Nguyen, the crew of a TV station in San Antonio, and the star of the show, *Hermana Luz* herself in bringing the miracle to pass. Their exile was sweetened considerably by the gold bars weighing down their luggage.

Most of the *Cristeros* returned to their homes, wondering privately how they'd gotten so swept up in the crusading fervor. Many of them got involved in hunting down the holdouts who wouldn't believe even *Hermana Luz* when she said the revolt was over.

Cipriano Fuentes became president of Mexico. There had been worse ones. His first official act was to cordially invite Powell Gooding to get his *gringo* ass north of the Rio Grande at his earliest convience, provided *right now* was convenient. For some reason the diplomat chose to take ship at Vera Cruz and

risk the pirates instead of following the letter of the president's
directive, which would have put him smack in the Republic of
Texas.

Even without him, the Texicans threw a helluva party.

They met on a hill apart from the festivities, which were
being held on President LaRousse's modest spread outside San
Antonio. It was a warm evening, and the stars were loose
overhead.

McKay held her hands for a moment, then, feeling the un-
familiar emotion of self-consciousness, let them go.

"I won't drag this out, Marla," he said. "But I thought you
oughta know . . . Steve's last words were of you. He, ah, said
to tell you he loved you."

She sobbed and suddenly she was hanging on to him, squeezing him so hard he thought his ribs might crack. He gazed off
in the general direction of the Big Dipper and stroked her golden
hair and tried not to be aware how damned good she felt pressed
up against him in her frilly off-the-shoulder dress.

When she had cried herself out she broke away, sniffled
once, and nodded. "Thank you," she whispered.

"Yeah." He nodded and turned away. "See you around."

"Where are you going, McKay?"

He shrugged. "Thought I'd leave you alone with your grief."
He thought of Tanya Jenkins, in Luxor, Iowa, long ago and
far away. "I know what it's like to lose a lover."

"A *lover?* Whatever are you talking about?"

He frowned. "Uh, well, Steve O'Neal."

"What on earth gave you the impression he was my lover?
The very idea."

"Well, ahh . . . I mean, I wasn't spying or anything, but at
the going-away party for us, I saw you kissing him."

"Of course you did. He was my cousin. We grew up together;
we were like brother and sister."

"Uh. Really. That's . . . that's very interesting."

"You're an idiot, McKay."

"Yeah. You're right."

She faced him with hands on hips. "Come here, you Yankee
son of a bitch. We got some unfinished business. Or did you

catch some godawful clap down in Mexico?"

"If anybody did, it wasn't me." He grinned. "And, come to think of it, I guess it ain't likely Case did, either."

"So what are you waiting for?"

"I can't think of any reason," he admitted, and came to her.